THE SCARECROWS

By Robert Westall

THE SCARE-CROWS

BY ROBERT WESTALL

GREENWILLOW BOOKS
New York

Library of Congress Cataloging in Publication Data
Westall, Robert.   The scarecrows.
Summary: While visiting his mother and new
stepfather whom he hates, an English teenager
is terrorized by three scarecrows embodying
people who met violent death and who silently
threaten the entire family.
[1. Remarriage—Fiction.   2. Stepfathers
—Fiction.   3. Horror stories]   I. Title.
PZ7.W51953Sc   [Fic]   81-2052
ISBN 0-688-00612-4   AACR2

For my friend Tony Collingford
who saw the scarecrows as well

1

IT WAS THE NIGHT before the Fund-raising Effort that the devils came. So it seemed to Simon Wood ever after.

But they were formless then.

They came with the whispering. There was always whispering in the dorm after lights out. But worse, the night before the parents came.

Chesworth was the night's first victim.

"Your father got *another* new car, Chesworth?"

Sniggers.

"Another *Vauxhall*, Chesworth?"

"Buys them in packs of ten, doesn't he, Chesworth?"

"Well, Vauxhalls are disposable, like bog rolls. Use 'em once, flush 'em down the bog, *don't* you, Chesworth?"

"Get your arse rusty!"

Not a sound from Chesworth. Any sound would only make things worse. Besides, this was routine stuff. Friend Bowdon just sharpening his teeth; getting warmed up for the evening's fun. Chesworth was lucky.

Bored, Bowdon passed to another routine victim.

"What's your mother wearing tomorrow, Riley?"

Silence.

"She came dressed as an Eskimo tart last time."

Silence.

"Smeared herself with whale blubber, an' all. What a pong."

Silence.

1

"Maybe she'll come as a Zulu virgin. Zulu virgins have rings through their. . . ."

Sniggers all down the rows of beds. Restrained, respectful sniggers. If you sniggered too loud, Bowdon might notice you. If you didn't snigger at all, he'd certainly notice.

Simon Wood didn't snigger.

Bowdon noticed. Simon felt him notice. Then felt him slither away again, into the dark. Bowdon was afraid of Simon. Bowdon was remembering the last time the parents came. Last summer's Parents' Day.

Simon remembered too.

Summer Parents' Day. Started all right. Mum had done nothing to shame him. Red hair short and clean, her make-up slight, her skirt a decent length. Her Morris Minor Traveller was nearly ten years old, but clean and shining. She hadn't tried to kiss him, just smiled and said hallo. Not even asked him if he was O.K. Nothing for Bowdon to overhear. Nothing for Bowdon to get his rotten little teeth into.

It was Montgomery's father who spoiled it. Montgomery's father, who used to play tennis for Gloucestershire. Montgomery's father with his lanky legs and bounding stride and crinkly black hair. Montgomery's father had buttonholed Mum. Somebody had cried off the parents' team who were playing tennis against the staff; would Mum step into the breach? Mum had fallen for it, like a sucker. Even though Simon begged her not to; with his eyes. Begged and *begged*. But Mum was always the willing sucker. . . .

Mum coming onto the court, beside Mr. Montgomery. In borrowed shorts. Showing her legs. Not that Mum's legs weren't all right. Not fat, with dimpled thighs and varicose veins like some mothers' legs. But when she bent over to pick up a ball, you could see her bottom.

Bowdon, and Bowdon's friend of the moment, and young Montgomery (who smashed anybody Bowdon wanted smashed), sitting on the grass by the umpire's chair. Looking at Mum's bottom as she picked up the balls. Muttering and laughing like they would make themselves sick, so that the Head, who was umpiring and doing his Wimbledon impersonation, turned round and glared at them three times. But they went on muttering and laughing.

Simon set his face like a rock—they were watching him too—and turned his mind off. There was a huge privet hedge round the court, because the school couldn't afford proper netting; it was full of the remains of crime. If you had something you wanted to hide, you held it inside your fist, plunged your fist into the hedge, and let go. The hedge was full of the sodden rags of ancient stolen caps, bleached exercise books from the sixties and torn nudey mags. Among which spiders spun and birds built their nests. It was a good place to hide your mind while you kept your face still as a rock, and the Head droned on about forty-love.

But he could still tell from the Head's voice that someone was losing pretty badly. It had to be Mum, because the staff pair were Slogger Newall and the games master, an Oxford blue. He raised his eyes in desperation above the hedge, to the tall willow trees. There was a hot gusty wind blowing up there, above the airless calm of the court. The trees leaned over, like people at a street accident. They looked as if they were going to fall, fall, as the savage gusts

3

lifted their leaves, showing the pale undersides in waves, like skirts.

"Advantage, Mrs. Wood," announced the Head. In spite of himself, Simon looked.

And there was Mum, up on her toes, spinning a crafty serve that sliced into the very corner. Slogger hit it thunderously into the net.

"Game to Mrs. Wood."

People clapping, even the school, as if they really meant it. And Mum standing there, cheeks pink and eyes shining, hair pulled back with an elastic band, looking no older than the sixth-form girls from down the road.

Simon had to watch after that, heart in his mouth with every stroke. Slogger and the games master and Mr. Montgomery all hit the ball hard. But Mum kept sticking her racket out at cunning angles, and the ball would vanish in a puff of chalk. And the school was all on Mum's side, because the games master was a cocky sod, and even Slogger was still a *teacher*. The waves of applause got bigger and bigger. . . .

"Game, set and match to Mrs. Wood and Mr. Montgomery!"

Mum was presented with a nickel-plated egg cup thing. As she took it from the Head she bent one knee and bobbed her head, and just for a moment Simon remembered being very small and watching Mum win at somewhere called Queen's Club, and Dad arriving from the War House, for some reason dressed in khaki and shining leather and moaning he was too late to see Mum win. Then the memory was gone, and Mum passed the egg cup back to the Head, so it could live in the dusty showcase for another year. Then they all had tea, and then—

Lights out. Whispering.

"I think your mother took *service* rather well," said Bowdon, greasy as a year-old *Playboy*.

For once, nobody sniggered. They were remembering how well Mum had played; they *liked* her. Somebody even said, "Knock it off, Bowdon," in muttered embarrassment.

But Bowdon went on. "She certainly knows how to handle a pair of balls."

The silence was absolute.

"And it was interesting, the way she bent down. . . ."

That was when the devils came.

Simon got out of bed without willing it. Felt the floor cold under his feet, like in a dream. Walked steadily across to Bowdon's bed. He knew he was being insane. Bowdon was twice his size; Bowdon would kill him.

Calmly, he reached for Bowdon in the dark, got hold of his pajama coat.

"Hey, what's up wi' you?" said Bowdon querulously.

Simon hit with all his strength.

He could remember nothing after that, except Bowdon wrenching and heaving under his hands, and Bowdon's pajamas tearing, and chairs falling and the iron pain of bed legs and slithering on the smooth polished floor and then . . . nothing.

Until he was standing in the washroom, with the lights on. Something was dripping off his nose and splashing on the floor. He looked down. There was a track of blood all down his pajamas, right to the crutch. And one of the toilet doors stood half-open with its lock smashed off. He gaped stupidly at the splintered star of bare wood in the blue door.

"Who did that?"

5

"You did, my lad," said a grim voice above his head: Slogger Newall's voice. Simon realized the strong hands holding him were Slogger's too. And the pale faces of the rest of the dorm were staring open mouthed from the washroom doorway.

A noise was coming from inside the toilet. A blubbering, punctuated by high-pitched hysterical intakes of breath. Craning sideways, he could see a pajama-clad form lying on the wet floor, curled round behind the toilet bowl, where the cleaner kept her toilet brush in its polythene holder.

"Who's that?"

Slogger's hands tightened round him. "You know bloody well who it is." Slogger's voice was a mixture of shock, severity and a tinge of grudging admiration.

"*Bowdon?*"

"Bowdon. Now go with Montgomery to the San."

In the San, Simon's nose went on bleeding till he never realized there was so much blood in the world. And it was Montgomery who made him lie back and did the stuff with wet hankies and keys at the back of the neck. Because Slogger and Matron had their hands full of Bowdon, beyond a closed door. Bowdon would not stop making that noise, until finally Matron gave him something.

"What *happened?*" croaked Simon. It was hard to make himself understood, because his throat kept filling with blood.

"Jeeze!" said Monty. "You were spraying snots of blood all over the place like a fire-breathing dragon. Bubbles. . . . An' he kept hitting you but you wouldn't stop. Can't you *remember* biting him? Then he ran into the toilet and started screaming an' Slogger came. . . . Don't you really remember anything?"

6

"No."

"You looked *potty*. Real bonkers. Like . . . like a Viking going . . . baresark in battle." Monty heaved a sigh at the effort this thought cost; he wasn't a very literary character. "Keep still or you'll start bleeding again."

Ever since then, Bowdon had been frightened of him. The whole dorm was; except Monty, who was frightened of nothing, and Tris la Chard, who was crazy anyway.

But nobody knew the worst thing: he was very frightened of himself.

Oh, they all still got at him, everyone but Monty and Tris. But only about one thing: about being insane; and that had a kind of nervous admiration which took away the sting. Nobody ever mentioned Mum, and that was all that mattered.

Three days later, the Head had him up in his study, and then couldn't find anything to say. Hummed and haahed about adolescence and glands and hormones, and then bumbled into silence, staring at his fake marble bust of Beethoven. Simon felt like blurting out, "Please, sir, am I really insane?" But that wasn't the kind of thing you asked the Head.

Eight months had passed, and it hadn't happened again. And now it was Fund-raising Effort, Easter Term. And Bowdon was sheering away from him into the dark, to torment others. Simon could feel the devils in the air around him now, making his legs ache with rigid stiffness and the palms of his hands sweat so he had to rub them dry on the sheets.

"Is your mother *fulfilled* at the moment, Harris?" asked Bowdon, gently, concernedly. Mrs. Harris was, in the outside world, a child psychiatrist. Not English. Austrian.

Voluble. Last summer, when the parents came, she'd talked to all the staff, on and on, about the need to give adolescent boys a sense of fulfillment. Bowdon overheard. Since that day, Harris had often wished he was dead.

"Harris? Harris? Speak to me when you're spoken to, boy! HARRIS HAAARRISSSSS!" This was the big one; the real victim of the night. Simon felt his hands, his back muscles tighten further, his scalp go prickly wet.

Somebody should kill Bowdon. Simon tried to think of a good reason for not killing Bowdon. Bowdon's mother would cry? Simon doubted it. Mrs. Bowdon didn't even bother to come to Parents' Day; nobody knew if she really existed. Bowdon was spawned out of a computer who'd been raped by a rattlesnake.

"HAAAAAAAARRRRIISSSSSSSS?" Bowdon's tone was almost affectionate.

Shall I? thought Simon. Shall I open my mind and let the devils in, and know nothing? Then it will all be over and Bowdon will be dead and we can all get some sleep. . . .

The domitory door opened suddenly; a shaft of yellow light cut along the parquet floor between the two rows of beds.

Was it Slogger? On night duty? Slogger could silence Bowdon; creeping silently up the stairs in his dark blue tracksuit, pouncing on Bowdon's bed, pouring a handy glass of water into it, while Bowdon squawked.

"Your bed's wet, Bowdon? You *dirty* boy! You'll have to remake it then, won't you?" Then Slogger would pull Bowdon's bed to pieces, strewing pillows and blankets the length of the dorm, draping a sheet from the lampshade, while the rest of the room bit the blankets not to laugh out loud.

Or Slogger saying, "Do me a favor, will you, Bowdon? Downstairs a minute?" Then he'd make Bowdon clean every old pair of rugger boots in the locker room, having kicked them round all the puddles in the yard first, all the dorm hanging out of the windows while Slogger kicked boots all over the place, shouting "Goal!" and Bowdon followed, mewing pathetically.

Oh yes, Slogger could silence Bowdon.

But it wasn't Slogger standing in the lighted doorway. It was Protheroe, the art master. So-called. Better known as the Old Goat. With his pathetic straggle of beard and his head sticking like a tortoise's out of the old blue duffle coat he wore even in warm weather. And his set-piece appeal to reason that he bleated like a goat or preached like the Archbishop of Canterbury, what was the difference? It had never been a great speech, even new. Now, everyone knew it by heart, and impersonations were no longer funny.

"Tonight," bleated the Old Goat, "I want a victory for common sense."

"Too late," muttered Monty. "They just lost ten-nil. To Brazil."

The Old Goat bleated on, straight through the snigger. "Tonight I want you to be reasonable. After all, you are the senior form in this . . . prep school."

"*Reasonable*," they all mocked in chorus under their breath, even Simon. So that there was an audible murmur.

"This dormitory is simply not getting enough sleep. Staff are complaining. The Head has mentioned it."

"*Complaining*," breathed the boys dreamily. "*Mentioned*."

"The overwhelming decent majority of you, who want to get enough sleep, who want to work hard at your lessons,

9

are being undermined by a small but malicious minority. It has got to stop, and I am going to stop it."

"*Stop it,*" breathed the dorm. Then, with a homosexual twist, "Oh, *stop* it."

Prothie paused to swallow nervously, and kept staring at the ceiling. He never looked at anybody; least of all the small but malicious minority.

On the other hand, Bowdon sat bolt upright in bed, beaming at Prothie with his Cheshire-cat grin, just yearning to be looked at. Straw-colored hair, rosy cheeks in a moon face, blue eyes like innocent, brilliant saucers.

"Bear it in mind," added Prothie. "You'll see it makes sense."

"Sir?" said Bowdon, sticking up a striped arm enthusiastically.

Prothie flicked off the lights and fled.

There was a moment's silence. Only the dim red light above the fire extinguisher remained. And the lights from the masters' wing gleaming through the uncurtained windows, where Prothie would be lighting up another fag with trembling fingers and counting desperately the hours and days to end-of-term, an unlooked-at *Life of Michelangelo* on his quivering knees. And the lights of passing cars, casting shadows of leafless trees that swept across the ceiling like jagged devil wings.

It was worse than before. While there'd been a chance that Slogger might burst in, there'd been a hope that things might not get too bad. But now they knew it was Prothie. . . . The whole dorm took a deep breath before changing gear. Again the devil wings from the headlights swept across the ceiling; the devils whispered in Simon's ears like the rush of blood. If he didn't know what he was doing, how could he be *blamed* for killing Bowdon? It was the fault of glands, hormones . . . blame the hormones. . . .

Blithely unaware of his doom, Bowdon continued down his primrose path.

"Haaarrissss!"

"HAAAAAAAAARRIS?"

"Harris's mother is a . . . um . . . lady of foreign extraction." The imitation of the Head's voice was perfect.

Snigger.

"Harris's mother is a lady of *German* extraction."

"A sodding Nazi?" offered Monty.

"Far from it, dear friends. She is . . . ah . . . erm . . . a lady of Hebrew descent. Her father was made into lampshades in the Sachsenhausen lampshade factory, well known to all our readers."

"I say, I say, I say, would you buy a used lampshade from Harris's grandmother?"

"They made him into soap, actually. They only made lampshades in Belsen."

Simon let the devils in. He felt them slide softly, lovingly into his muscles. The tension was going. He felt yards above himself, far away, up near the dark ceiling. Unreal, lovely. He put one foot to the cold floor. It had always been inevitable, Bowdon and him. . . .

Then, from the far end of the dorm, came a giggle. Not a snigger. A genuine, happy giggle, from the land of sanity, from the world outside. Everybody looked that way. In the corner, somebody's bedclothes were elevating like a dim mushroom cloud. Then the cloud collapsed in the middle, and moved down the bed, humping itself like a caterpillar.

11

Everyone was giggling now.

"What you doing, Tris, you mad sod?" shouted someone.

A muffled voice came from the humped bed. "Looking for me Smarties."

"What they doing down there, Tris?"

"Put them in me bedsocks to hatch." The bed leaped up and down. "Christ, they hatched. They're *biting!*"

"Biting where, Tris?"

"Never you bloody mind!" screamed Tris in a shrill falsetto. He gave an agonized shriek and came flailing down the room, wrapped tightly in his blankets.

"Oh, shut up, you stupid idiot," said Bowdon crossly, his game with Harris ruined. But nobody listened to Bowdon, once Tris bust loose. Everybody was falling about; even Harris.

"Ay'm the Sheik of Araby, and up your oil well I'll creep," yodeled Tris. Somehow the blankets had become a flowing burnoose. Then he went into his Mad Monk routine, intoning the Pythagorean Theorem with all the sanctity of High Mass. He had just reached "*Quod Erat Demonstrandum*" and the dorm replied "Amen," when Prothie burst in again. Once Prothie realized he only had Tris to deal with, and not Bowdon, Prothie really played the Big Hero. As a result of which, Tris would be up in front of the Head in the morning.

When Prothie went, Bowdon tried to start on Harris again. But the dorm had laughed too much, and they were angry about Tris being in trouble.

"Aah, shut your face, Bowdon," muttered a brave soul, far down the room.

"Who was that?" asked Bowdon nastily.

"Everybody," said everybody; and, yawning, slept.

2

SIMON LAY on his neatly made bed, reading *Watership Down*. Always *Watership Down* when he felt jumpy. Practically knew it by heart.

Sun shone through the windows, scouring away the filth and dreams of the night. There were curtains at the windows, but they hung in rigid folds. It was a tradition that the senior dorm never drew them; drawn curtains reminded you of the softness of home. Drawing your curtains would have made you different from the others. Different was dangerous. Matron took down the curtains to wash them every summer holiday. Between times, spiders spun tiny webs inside the stiff folds.

Bowdon, and everybody else whose parents weren't coming, had gone down to the gates, to have a good laugh at other people's parents driving in. People whose parents were coming hung around the dorm, restless. Waiting for a word; keeping as far from Bowdon as possible.

Simon had his father on his bedside locker. In an unspectacular black frame, ten inches by eight. Father looked thirty years old and very alive. He would never get any older.

Father looked hard, a horseman. Handsome, except that his skull, under Brylcreemed hair, was rather too narrow. That is how Father would have seemed to an outsider.

Simon never thought like that. He remembered his father as huge, towering. Lifting Simon up on his shoulder and spinning him till the ceiling whirled. Then putting Simon down and laughing, while Simon tottered, dizzy, on short legs from chair to table, clinging on desperately.

13

Father was a shining man; kept shining by a Cockney soldier called Corporal Briggs. Simon could clearly remember Corporal Briggs; cropped hair and the constant smell of *Brasso* and singeing khaki cloth. Oh, and he could talk with a cigarette in his mouth, because he could make the cigarette stick to his lower lip. The cigarette wagged up and down, while Corporal Briggs told Simon of a magic place called the Western Desert, and a wizard called Old Rommel who could make tanks and men suddenly appear out of nowhere. Sometimes the cigarette stuck to Corporal Briggs's lip a bit too well, and he would have to pull it off by force, and a bit of his lip would come off with it.

Corporal Briggs polished Father's car as well. So that you could see your own face all moony and dark, peering out at you from the green paint; or all bendy and wobbly in the silver headlights. The car was vintage and had a big leather strap to fasten down the bonnet. When the engine was running, you couldn't hear it, but if you put your hand on the bonnet you could feel it buzzing inside like a huge bee, and the edge of the windscreen shivered into a blur. Once, Father took him out alone in the car and kept shouting, "Shall we go faster, Simon?" and Simon kept yelling, "Faster, faster!" and every time he yelled "Faster," Father got more pleased, and the road beyond the car door flew past, so close that Simon could have put out his hand and touched it. And the seats smelled all leather, like Corporal Briggs polishing Father's shoes till they shone like new conkers.

Father was all shiny leather and brass, and when he picked you up and hugged you, the brass bits stuck into you, but you didn't mind. And you could undo the button

14

on his leather belt and there was a revolver, dark blue and smelling of oil.

Father was always appearing in the funniest places. Once, Mum said, "Let's go and see him," and they went to a big field, full of people who blocked out the sky till Mum picked him up; but there was no sign of Father. All the people were licking ice creams and playing radios, and there were big trumpets up on sticks and a loud voice coming through them that echoed, echoed, echoed. But there was still no sign of Father, and Simon could not see how Father could possibly get through the crowd because it was now so thick. Airplanes kept flying very low, and the crowd kept screaming, but Simon could tell they were enjoying themselves really, because they didn't run away. And the echoing voice kept going on about the clouds overhead which were thick and moving fast in the wind.

Then suddenly there was a blue gap in the clouds, and a plane with two engines, and the sky was full of red and white roses, blossoming mysteriously behind the plane. And Mum said, "There's Daddy now, at the front because he has to make sure all the other men jump before he does." Simon didn't believe that Father was up in the sky with the rose, because the rose was so small. But it got bigger and bigger, then vanished behind the crowd; and suddenly there was Father laughing and kissing Mum, even though he had his arms full of red stuff in a great bundle, and a red helmet on his head, so he seemed more like a monster on the telly.

"Ey," said Tris la Chard, standing at the foot of Simon's bed with a towel round his neck. "Your mum's here."

There was something in Tris's voice Simon didn't like. Not spite; Tris was never spiteful. But it could have been

15

concern, and that was more scaring. He looked at Tris carefully. Tris didn't look back, but began strangling himself with the towel. Only Tris could hold his hands and twist his face so that you could swear there was somebody standing behind him, strangling him.

"What do you mean, my mum's here?"

Tris had a bean-shaped face and a bean-shaped nose, and black hair that stuck out all over the place. He kept his eyes down now, hiding them behind his hair.

"She came with a guy in a white Range Rover. New. A beaut."

Terror seized Simon, but he kept his voice calm and said, "You mean she's *talking* to a guy in a white Range Rover?"

"No. She came inside it. Bowdon. . . ."

Silence. But Tris went on hanging around trying to strangle himself. Finally he said sorrowfully, "The guy's not . . . the guy's a. . . ."

"A yob," said Simon, closing his eyes. He heard Tris go on down the form, kicking the legs of the beds. The devils whispered softly in his ears. He watched himself put one foot to the floor after the other. Walked downstairs, ice cold.

The white Range Rover was parked under the trees beside the coach house, with all the other cars. Lots of parents standing around talking, waiting for the Head to appear and the money screwing to begin. Boys with parents there were standing on the bumpers of new cars, or thumping their kid sisters. All very normal, except there was a gap in the middle around the Range Rover, Mum and a man. The other parents had sort of turned their backs and were talking and laughing so hard you would think they were being paid by the word. And giving sly glances over their shoulders at the Range Rover and Mum and the man.

He was a yob. No tie. Wide sloping shoulders like a navvy. Huge hands and a beer paunch. Not a very big paunch; he was really all slabby muscle like Slogger. But Slogger kept himself pulled in, and this guy let it all hang out like he was pregnant and didn't care who knew it. Wearing white trousers and a white safari jacket and a dark blue shirt. His nose was big and had spots on it and hair growing inside his nostrils. Thick lips and balding, with a big black beard.

"The guy's head's on upside down," observed Bowdon, from the fringes of the crowd. All Bowdon's mates sniggered. So did some parents, though very quietly.

Mum was worried, glancing round, biting her lip; she knew she'd dropped one. But the yob couldn't care less. He was staring around with a smirk; eyes slightly narrowed. Finding the school and the parents just as funny as they were finding him, as if he had a right to be there, and they hadn't. He pointed to something high on the coach house, and Mum laughed suddenly and looked better. Simon looked where they were looking. The mellow old Georgian walls of the coach house were topped by cheap plastic guttering. It did look peculiar, but the school couldn't *afford* better.

The yob was laughing at the school; making Mum laugh.

Simon nearly walked away there and then. But Mum had seen him. She caught his eye and silently commanded him to walk over. There was no arguing with her in that mood, so he went. Feeling Bowdon's eyes, everybody's eyes, on the back of his neck.

17

"Hallo," said Mum, blue eyes full of don't-you-dare. "This is Joe Moreton. He drove me down."

Simon shook hands. Moreton's hand was warm and dry and he didn't try the old crushing technique. But Simon couldn't get his own hand away quick enough.

"Where's the Morris?" asked Simon, too loud.

"A gasket went. I'd just called in at the gallery. Mr. Moreton was there. He very kindly offered to drive me, or I wouldn't be here."

Then, disastrously, there was nothing more to say. Simon could tell Mum was trying to think of something, but she wasn't going to manage it.

"Is there a gents?" asked Joe Moreton suddenly. "Before I die?"

Stammering, Simon pointed it out. Everybody had heard Joe Moreton ask. . . .

Joe ambled off.

"Who *is* he?" asked Simon, in a screeching whisper.

"Stop flapping. Just an artist from the gallery. I hardly know him. I was just going to ring the school to say I couldn't make it, when he offered. Show some manners. If it wasn't for him I shouldn't be here."

Simon nearly said he wished she wasn't.

Joe Moreton ambled back, surveying everything with an artistic eye. Especially the younger mothers. They gave him frosty looks, but he just leered.

Again, there was nothing to say.

But now old Protheroe was hovering nearer and nearer, with a beatific smile like he'd seen God and lived. He paused at two yards' range and waved his hands as if he was conducting an invisible fairy orchestra. Kept grinning fatuously and trying to catch *somebody's* eye. Bowdon and co. were having their best time since the cricket pavilion burned down.

"Yes, Mr. Protheroe?" said Mum, with a worse edge to her voice than Prothie normally got.

Protheroe really did look like he'd reached Nirvana. Simon decided it was all a bad dream; he'd wake up in a minute.

"It is Joe Moreton, isn't it? *The Observer? Private Eye?*" asked Prothie.

"It is," said Joe Moreton gently.

Prothie took his hand and wouldn't put it down. Kept shaking it vaguely. "I do so admire your work, sir. Tradition of the great English cartoonists . . . Hogarth . . . Gilray . . . Rowlandson. . . ."

"Oh, I wouldn't say that."

"I never miss a *thing* you do. That one of the Chancellor. . . ."

Joe Moreton smiled sickly, and regained possession of his own hand by main force.

"*So* nice. Such a privilege. . . ." Prothie wandered off through the crowd, telling complete strangers all about his great privilege.

Bowdon was in danger of doing himself a permanent injury. All Bowdon's mob were mouthing, "*So* nice . . . such a privilege."

But the parents weren't laughing. They were starting to turn and give Joe Moreton the same daffy looks as Protheroe. As if Protheroe was spreading a mental Black Death or something. The parents closed in. Mr. Montgomery shook Joe Moreton's hand and began telling him how he

19

used to play for Gloucester and did Joe come from those parts? Another man introduced his wife like she was the Crown Jewels, and the wife put her hand on Moreton's arm and said he must come over to Blackheath for dinner one day.

And then, to crown the madness, there was the Head, welcoming the well-known Joe Moreton among us, and would he consider judging the art exhibition as there were small prizes for first and second? (From the look on Prothie's face, it was news to him, because the Head was normally so stingy about art that there was never even enough paper.) And perhaps one day Mr. Moreton would consider doing a little picture for the school?

Simon felt like throwing up.

But Joe Moreton just stood smiling; though you could tell he was laughing at them all inside. Then he held up a hand, saying, "Headmaster, your word is my command! Just stay exactly where you are."

And the Head stood exactly where he was, one hand on the wing of the white Range Rover; the cold wind blowing his scant gray hair across his bald patch and pressing his gown and trousers hard against his ridiculously spindly legs. Stood with a fixed smirk on his face until he was shivering with cold.

Joe Moreton reached through the window of his car and produced Biro and a large spiral-backed sketchbook. It was then that Simon saw for the first time the strange and hateful talent of Joe Moreton. The Biro seemed to move of its own accord, rolled, stippled, slashed. A horrible mess of lines. Pure rubbish, thought Simon. Now they'll find him out, the yob.

But slowly, out of the slashed scribbles, an image of the Head emerged. Bald head, spindle shanks, paunchy tum under its gray waistcoat. The drawing made him look tiny, like an aggressive robin. So real you had to laugh. Except Moreton showed more than was there: the tension in the clenched hand on the wing of the car; the Head's desperation under the politeness he always showed to rude, bullying parents. Moreton stripped the Head naked. And the Head stood there smirking, loving every minute.

The parents loved it too; craning their necks and pushing for a view. Giving little gasps of wonder, like tots at a Punch and Judy show. When Moreton finished, there was a round of applause, as if someone had scored a century. Couldn't they see how cruel it was? Couldn't they see that underneath, Moreton was mocking them all?

The rest of the day passed in a horrible blur. Simon played scrum-half for the school against Riverside College. Played savagely, to forget. But every time he put the ball into the scrum, he wondered if Joe Moreton was watching, turning him into a ridiculous figure with his bottom stuck in the air and hands clenched too tight on the ball.

Simon scored two tries, and was twice spoken to for dangerous play. Later, the drawing of the Head was auctioned for the Science Lab Fund. Mr. Montgomery made the top bid—a hundred pounds.

It was just sick.

3

SIMON SAT WATCHING the telly in a paroxysm of hatred and boredom. He loathed the smarmy, crinkle-haired good looks of the quiz master; the pretty, permanently grinning girls; and the aging couples willing to strip their lives naked for thirty pounds and the inevitable silver clock. Simon had the telly sound down, because Mum was going out *again*. He could hear her footsteps overhead in her bedroom, moving in quick bursts from wardrobe to dressing table. She was singing too. Happy.

Not that he didn't want her to be happy. Happy with him and Jane. But she was too happy these days, and it was about something else. Two days a week she was up early, before he got up; getting ready to go to work at the gallery. She would come in to say good-bye, checking that she had her watch and her car keys and her purse, and looking at herself in the mirror over his bed, her mind already miles away. And she'd bought a lot of new clothes. Frilly blouses and frilly skirts that she wore over leather boots.

And four times in three weeks she'd gone out in the evening; and the house was thick with old programs for weird-looking plays at the Roundhouse, and concerts with names like Monteverdi and Albinoni. And there were the hour-long phone calls, almost nightly, when she closed the door of the study and emerged all shining and pink and was in a good humor for the rest of the evening. But she was a bit snarly on the nights the phone call didn't come.

He didn't mind staying home in the day and looking after Jane and doing her bangers and beans for lunch. There'd never been anybody much to knock around with in the holidays anyway, unless Tris came to stay. But Mum used to take him and Jane out. To Battersea Park, or the Science Museum. Mind you, she still did. But she was always wanting to try new places now, even the prating Tate Gallery once. And her mind was never quite on it.

He would almost be glad to get back to school.

And Jane, when she wasn't playing in the garden with her little council schoolmates, or bossing her tatty dolls in the wendy house, or chucking slime out of the goldfish pond, would sometimes mention a character called Uncle Bear. Jane was very keen on Uncle Bear. Uncle Bear had taken her to the zoo and lifted her on his shoulders so she could see the giraffes properly. Only, when he asked who Uncle Bear was, she got sly and changed the subject. Simon had a growing terror that Uncle Bear might be Joe Moreton. On the other hand, he could be her teacher at school or *anything*. . . . Simon couldn't quite bring himself to pry deeper. Spying on Mum through Jane was not on; and Jane's eyes were too knowing.

Mum came downstairs, pulling on gloves. "All right, dear? Shan't be late. There's yogurts in the fridge. Try to get Jane in bed by eight. And don't let her get dirty after her bath." Mum looked all lit up again. "Mrs. Logan will look in, in case you need anything."

Simon was getting awfully tired of Mrs. Logan next door. She never seemed to go out anywhere. Just stayed home asking nosy questions and playing old Glenn Miller records, and talking to her fat spaniel dog. He wanted to shout at Mum, "Where are you *going?* Who *with?*" But he couldn't quite bring himself to do it.

23

Mum said, "Mrs. Logan's got a phone number in case. . . ." She paused with her hand on the door handle. "Would you like to come to the gallery tomorrow, Simon? We've got a new exhibition opening. Lots of nosh for the customers—mini pork pies and things. You might enjoy it. I'd like you to see where I work. I do feel I've been neglecting you these holidays . . . a bit. . . ."

He looked at her. Couldn't quite read the look on her face. Just guilty conscience . . . or a bit slyer than that?

"No," he said abruptly. "You *know* I don't like paintings."

"Suit yourself. Anyway, I won't be late."

After she'd gone, he felt restless. Switched the telly from channel to channel, then switched off in disgust. But that made the house too silent. Even if Jane and her fiendish mates were screaming over a flaming pussy cat in the garden. So he switched it back on, and went and ate three yogurts in the kitchen.

Then he prowled around the house. It was still exactly as he remembered: the rose wallpaper in the diningroom; the can opener grinding loosely on its moorings on the kitchen wall. But it all seemed empty, unreal. Even the poplars at the bottom of the garden, bathed in evening sunlight, seemed like something on the telly. Because Mum wasn't there. Mum wasn't there, even when she was there. . . .

He *would* go to the gallery tomorrow; he must find out what was going on.

He wore his suit. What he and Mum called laughingly his chapel-and-weddings suit. He didn't much like weddings. And he had once worn it at Granny's house; waiting for them to come back from Granny's funeral. And when they all came back they were horrible; horribly jolly. Like aristocrats in the French Revolution keeping up their spirits and all the time wondering who was next for the chop.

Worse, he had to wear last summer's chapel-and-weddings suit, which was halfway up his wrists and ankles; and a white shirt that was too tight.

As soon as they got to the gallery, Mum's boss grabbed her. A dark man called Gluck, with tight curly hair and a purple shirt, who was frantic about what a man called Higginson would think. Mum reassured him that Higginson was quite human if plied with enough to drink. Then she was busy answering the phone, laying out row on row of puff pastry things and opening bottles of wine while Gluck merely flapped his hands around. She did find time to push a catalogue into Simon's hand, give him a shove toward the gallery proper and say, "Go and *enjoy* yourself; keep an open mind!"

Simon drifted into the gallery proper. It was empty, except for pictures. Simon took one look at the pictures, screamed, "Oh, *no!*" and flung the catalogue the whole length of the room. Then he ran and picked it up quickly again, before Mr. Gluck could notice.

All the pictures were by Joe Moreton. There was one of the Prime Minister, and one of the Chancellor of the Exchequer. Horrible. The Chancellor of the Exchequer was made up from a jumble of dollar signs and trade graphs. Behind him was the Bank of England, all falling down and twisted. It was just a jumble of pen strokes close to, but if you stepped back it looked just like him, as he appeared on the telly. All efficient and sensible on top, and dead scared underneath. All Joe Moreton's people looked scared underneath, like the people at Granny's funeral. It made you feel scared yourself; as if nothing in the world was what it seemed. If Joe Moreton drew Jesus Christ, he'd make him out of thorns and nails; saving the world on the surface and as scared as hell underneath. Things like that should be a crime. People like Joe Moreton should be put in prison.

The gallery filled up with potential customers who mostly walked past Mum as if she wasn't there and dived for the silver trays of pale wine. Then they turned their backs on the pictures and began shouting at each other that they'd been to Afghanistan for their holidays and barely escaped with their lives. Or walked through Central Park every night and no mugger had dared lay a finger on them. One bald guy, who had only been to New Zealand at the firm's expense, kept on saying weren't the New Zealand trees *oppressive?* Nobody listened to anybody; just tried screaming the loudest.

Simon made his way to the grub and began hammering the pork pies, seeing how many he could stuff down before they ran out. Nobody else seemed to be eating; just boozing and saying they'd met the Dalai Lama in Kashmir and wasn't he a *dear*, but a born loser, poor man, too good for this world. Simon ate seventeen pies and then gave up, feeling sick. Everyone went on stubbing everyone else out, and the room got fuller and fuller of people bigger than himself. Who didn't hear, the first time he asked to get past them; didn't hear till the third time when he shouted, and then said, "Dear *me*," and backed away to let him through as if he were a leper or something. Somebody asked, "Who *is* that child?"

The gallery became so full he had nowhere left to go. He

26

looked for Mum, but she was busy sticking red spots on pictures, which meant they'd been sold. Mum had to bend down to do it, and one guy passing patted her bottom. Mum gave an annoyed wriggle, but the guy went on patting her till she slid off somewhere, with the guy in pursuit.

The devils began to whisper in his ears, among the noise and the fag smoke.

He blundered after Mum, but lost her. Blundered into Joe Moreton himself, smiling his sneer and saying a few words every so often. Half a dozen guys wrote down everything Joe said, holding notebooks and glasses in one hand and Biros in the other so that every time they wrote, wine spilled down their notebooks; but they were too sloshed to care.

Joe Moreton saw him and said, "Hi, Simon!" For some reason Simon thought Joe's eyes went soft, kind . . . but he just pushed past rudely and back into the crowd. He suddenly felt appallingly thirsty; too much salt in the pork pies. He'd like a glass of water, but there was no water. In desperation he grabbed a glass of yellow wine off a tray and drank it in one swig. It tasted like flat, bitter water, so he had three more.

So *hot!* Fag smoke made his eyes sting. He rubbed them, but that made them ten times worse; he couldn't keep them open and tears were streaming down his face. God, they would think he was *crying!*

Head spinning. Or the room or something. He looked desperately for a place to hide . . . went round the room three times more. Just when he was thinking he would go on walking forever, like one of Jane's electric robots, he saw a place.

A set of screens stuck out into the room, to make an interesting shape. There was a gap between one screen and the wall of the gallery. It had been masked by a rubber plant and a drape of orange curtain, but the curtain had sagged on its drawing pins.

A quick look around the room. Every back was turned to him. A thin blonde woman had managed to spill her booze down her oyster-colored suit, and a tall guy was mopping her with a large handkerchief and a lot of enthusiasm. The blonde was swaying her hips and everyone else was jeering them on.

Simon slipped through the curtain, into a tiny world of his own. There was a clutter of things: broken picture frames, a hammer and nails, a yogurt jar of pins and an old wooden chair well spattered with paint. He sat on the chair and picked up a catalogue from a very dusty pile. It was nearly a year out of date, about a show of sculpture made from plastic ducks and surgical tubing. By a guy called Yuri Malinowski who'd been an engine driver on the Trans-Siberian railway, then a shark fisherman, then Professor of Ecology at Berkeley, California. His sculptures were a protest against the artificiality of modern ecostructures.

Simon put down the catalogue. The screens subdued the noise of the room to a buzz, like a hive of narky bees. They cut off the sight of everybody, except legs and feet. Which made them deliciously ridiculous. He sat watching the feet, and guessing which voices belonged to which feet.

At the moment, there was a pair of well-muscled female legs attached to cherry red walking shoes with thick sensible soles. Talking to a pair of possibly male legs in small-checked trousers. Possibly male, because the two voices were uncannily alike. Deep-pitched for a woman, but pouf-fish for a man. . . . Spiteful voices.

28

"Rotten exhibition," said Cherry-shoes. "Just selling off his old drawings from the newspapers. Three hundred quid for *that*."

"If there are fools who'll pay his price. . . ."

"Germans and Japs."

"Fair swap—a secondhand Joe Moreton for a lousy Jap color telly. Makes me sick the way the Japs ape Western culture. Golf, rugby, ballroom dancing."

"Wonder how much they'd give for the Royal Family . . . that'd stop the yen crisis for a bit."

"Not on your life. They'd flood the market in a year, with full-sized transistorized walking models of the Duke of Edinburgh—a sort of Action Duke."

"Who's that weird kid? The one with the suit and the short back and sides? Like something out of *Tom Brown's Schooldays*."

"Haven't you *heard!*" The voice rose to a scream of delight. "He's Moreton's girlfriend's brat."

"The red-haired bit? *That's* not still on . . . ?"

"Hotter and *hotter*."

"Can't see what he sees in her. Beyond the usual."

"Oh, there's been none of the *usual*. He hasn't laid a *finger* on her yet. Could have had her for the lift of an eyebrow; she's *panting* for it. But that's not our Joe's way. It's marriage or nothing for our Joe."

"Why, for God's sake?"

"Our Joe's your original northern puritan. Or you might say. . . ."

"Yes?" The voice was avid.

"They say he's a salt miner's son from Cheshire. Ever since he hit the big time, he's been collecting antiques. Owns half a stately home. Maybe he wants her as the jewel of his

29

collection. Brigadier's daughter's a big status symbol. A well-stuffed memsahib to hang on the wall . . . like the tigers her daddy shot. Apparently she's willing to sleep with him, but not to marry him. But I can't see her holding out much longer. Hot little lady, that one. Goes with the red hair."

They drifted away, discussing a new book that exposed T. S. Eliot as the spiritual bank clerk he really was.

They had been talking about *Mum*.

Eventually, the voices in the gallery scattered and died. No more feet appeared under the screens. Mr. Gluck could be heard rejoicing to the tune of nine thousand six hundred pounds, and reckoning up his own share of the commission.

Simon sat on behind the screen, still as a stone.

Then he heard Mum say sharply, "I can't find him anywhere, Joe."

"Can't have gone far," said Joe soothingly. His voice was different when he was alone with Mum. No sneer. All warm and gooey and utterly repulsive.

"Joe, I'm worried."

"Well, Charlie on the door said he didn't go out. And he can't have vanished into thin air . . . so if you rule out the impossible, then what remains, however unlikely. . . ."

The screen swung back, and the pair of them were standing there. That was the first time Simon ever thought of them as "the pair."

They all stared at each other silently. The devils had Simon by the throat. He couldn't have uttered a word if he died for it. The silence got longer and longer, and then Mum reached forward and shook him by the shoulder.

"Simon. *Simon!* Whatever's the matter with you?"

Silence still growing. If I open my mouth an inch, thought Simon, I shall never stop shouting till I'm dead.

Then Joe reached forward and picked a wine glass off the floor, and sniffed it. "He's pissed, the little bastard. Slewed as a newt." He laughed, at his own cleverness. "Here, I'll carry him down to the car."

"Don't *touch* me!" shouted Simon.

Joe backed away, a baffled look on his hairy face. Then suddenly, without a thing being said, everybody knew that everybody knew. Mum was as white as a sheet; even Joe's great hairy face looked pale.

"Then you'll move yourself. Or I'll move you," said Mum. Her face was white as a burning bone now, under the red hair. She grabbed his shoulder, and for the first time in his life, her hand hurt him.

"I'll drive you home," said Joe in a shaky voice.

They put Simon in the back of the Range Rover and drove home to Croydon. He sat, trying not to touch the sides of the filthy car; trying to get inside himself so he didn't even have to sit on its filthy seat. Hating the clutter in the back; the ragged sketchbooks, the muddy wellingtons, the tattered programs for the Roundhouse and Vivaldi and Albinoni. . . . Trying not even to breathe the car's air, as the rain came down and the windows steamed up, and the smell of Joe Moreton, animal and yobbish and reeking of French cigarettes, crept into his nostrils.

The pair were silent in the front; but they still kept looking at each other.

31

4

A LITTLE KID came into the classroom with a note.

"Wood?" said Slogger. "The Head wants to see you. Not in his study; in his house."

The whole class drew in its breath, sharply. Study was bad; almost certainly a walloping. But house was worse. In the house you learned that your father had dropped down dead of a heart attack; or your mother run off with another man.

The square of gravel between school and house glistened under the May sun, polished by a recent shower. Peaceful; various hums from various classes through various windows. First-years trying "Morning Has Broken" with shrill, sweet voices, only to be stopped by the music master and grumbled at after two lines. Morning certainly broke pretty quickly round here. . . .

His footsteps crunched loud and lonely on the gravel. There was a blue Renault 5 parked in front of the Head's house. Nobody Simon knew.

Had something happened to Mum?

But Mum was sitting in the Head's best chair. Only nervous; because she had her knees tight together and her handbag perched on top, and her hands kept undoing the clasp. She'd let her hair grow longer so it was neither one thing nor the other. Her grin was trying too hard.

Old Smily the Head was nervous too. On his feet like greased lightning, making gentle pushing motions with his hands toward the door. Old Smily not wanting to get involved. "Your mother has come to take you out to tea,

Wood. Lucky lad! What lessons have you got for the rest of the afternoon?"

"Only RK with you, sir."

"*Only* RK with me," mused Old Smily. "See what we ushers have to put up with, Mrs. Wood? *Only* RK with me. Ah well. . . ."

Moving sideways, like an obsequious crab, he opened his study door even wider. "Have a pleasant time. A good *chat*. If there's anything else, Mrs. Wood, perhaps you'd give me a ring . . . ?"

Outside, Simon said abruptly, "Where's the car?"

Mum unlocked the doors of the Renault. It was show-room-shiny, with polythene covers still on the seats.

"Where's the Morris?"

"Sold it. We had to have a change sometime. Heavens, Simon, the Morris was *ancient*."

"But this isn't big enough for holidays. We can't get all the stuff in *this*."

"Oh, we can use the—" She paused, bit her lip. "Let's go and have some tea."

"We can use *what?*" shouted Simon. His mind was full of a big white Range Rover.

Mum didn't answer. Instead, she began asking about school. Lots of questions that had nothing to do with each other. Stupid questions. Questions to which she already knew the answers. Simon grunted back in monosyllables. The new-plastic smell inside the car was choking him like poison gas.

"Please can we stop? I feel sick."

Mum pulled up, and savagely applied the handbrake. Then they sat side by side, staring down the sunlit road, while a cold gap grew between them; sort of hovering over the gear shift. When the gap grew so big that it seemed it must burst the car into a thousand pieces, Mum said:

"I'm going to get married again, Simon."

"To him? Not to *him!*"

"Yes." They didn't have to mention any names.

"But why, why, WHY? We're O.K. as we are. We're fine."

"You were fine, Simon. I was lonely." She was biting her lip again. But her bosom swelled softly, and her knees were small and shiny beneath her skirt. Mothers shouldn't look like that.

"*Why* were you lonely? You've got Jane. And Auntie Marge and Nunk and Auntie Mabel. And . . . your job."

"That's not the same."

"Did *he* buy you this car?"

"No, Simon, no. I sold some shares."

"My father's shares."

"No. Some your grandfather left me, that had nothing to do with Daddy. Anyway, what's the car got to do with it? Stop being silly. Let's go and have some tea."

She restarted the car. Outside, the sunlit country slid past. Cows stared, dogs barked; two women talking at a gate turned to look at them incuriously, heartlessly, as they stopped for a halt sign. Inside the car the cold swelled and swelled again. He kept on swallowing it, as it poured down his throat.

"Please stop the car, I feel sick again."

"Simon. This is *ridiculous*." But she stopped. He got out and faced into the hedge and a signpost saying *Swindon 2*. Trying to be sick. But he only managed an enormous belch that left a rotten taste in his mouth, and a few strings of saliva on the tall, dusty roadside weeds. When he turned back, Mum was looking at him, dead worried. Her look somehow made the big cold thing go away. He didn't really hate her; she was Mum. He felt he had just been very ill, or insane, but he was better now. It was going to be all right. She held out her hand to him; the one with the wedding ring he used to turn round and round her finger when he was small.

He took her hand now, turned the ring gently and said, "Please don't marry him. Please. I really couldn't bear it. I don't care what else you do—when I'm not around. But *please* don't marry him." He lowered his head in a kind of surrender. She ruffled his hair with her other hand.

"I didn't come to ask you if I could marry him. I've given him my word and that's *settled*. I came to ask you about . . . arrangements."

"But if you marry him, I can't come home. Ever."

She tightened her lips. "That's one of the things we've got to talk about. I'm selling the house, and Jane and I are moving to Cheshire. I need to know what things you want to keep and. . . ."

He didn't think it could have got any worse, but it did. He just kept staring at his shoes. At the great big scrape mark he'd made on one toe, playing football after lunch in the yard. An hour ago I was happy and I didn't even know I was happy. . . .

"Your hamsters—"

"Give them away. Give them to Billy Turner." Billy Turner was the char's son. Cruel; always trying to interfere with the hamsters. Mum had spoken to him about it. It was like sending your two best friends to the torture chamber.

"Perhaps that would be best," said Mum, relieved. "It would have been difficult in the removal van. We can buy you some more there."

We? We? He no longer knew who "we" was.

"Who's we?" he asked, head still down.

"Simon, don't be silly. I thought you were beginning to be sensible. What about your model railway?"

"Sell it. Give it away. Give that to Billy Turner too. Throw it out of the window."

She tried to take his hand again, but he shook her off. "Simon, look. I haven't got much time. I had to take a day off work specially. I've driven a hundred miles . . . I have to be back by seven . . . *please* be sensible. I only want to know if there are any things you don't want any more. We can take them all if you like. There'll be room. And the hamsters, they can easily go in the back of the Range Rover."

Her mouth was shaking. This is the way, he thought. This is the way to smash it.

"Give everything away," he said; and when his voice caught in his throat by accident he was not displeased. "And write to Nunk and ask if I can stay with him this summer holiday, till I go to Wellington."

"But you've invited Tris to stay with us again!"

"Tris—at *his* house? Joe Moreton's rotten house? You must be joking. I invite friends to *our* house."

"But Tris—"

"If you're so fond of Tris, you should have thought. . . ."

She was silent a long time; he thought he'd won. Then she said, in her steeliest voice, "Either you stop these silly games, Simon, or I'm taking you back to school. I've given

Joe my word, and you know I always keep my word. I know it's hard for you. That's why I came all this way to tell you myself. I could have written you a letter. I'll do anything to make it up to you, you know I will, but—"

"Take me back to school!"

"Is that what you really want?"

"Yes."

She waited another moment, then turned the key in the ignition and did a precise three-point turn, and drove toward school in silence. School got nearer and nearer. Every bend and halt sign, he was expecting her to give in. But at last they arrived. Classes had just ended. He saw Bowdon and . . . and Tris. Tris waved to Mum, and pretended to fall into a flower bed. Mum waved back and laughed out loud.

That laugh did it. He got out of the car in a flash. Mum wound down the car window swiftly, and even then for a crazy moment he thought he'd won. But she only asked the same stupid questions.

"So you don't want to come home for the wedding?"

"No."

"And you don't want to keep the hamsters?"

"No."

"Or any things?"

"No."

Each no was like the blow of a hammer. Smashing. Knocking down. Every time, she winced. But she kept on to the end. In a miserable black way, he loved it; loved the smashing up like he was drunk. But sometime, it had to come to an end.

"Good-bye for now, Simon. I'll write to you soon; even if you don't write back."

"They make us write home, didn't you know?"

It was amazing how you could go on hurting people.

"Isn't there anything you want to keep?"

"Yeah. My father's army kit."

Mum's eyes went as small as pins.

"It's *mine!*" he shouted. "He left it to me in his will. All personal possessions. It *said*. I have to choose on my twenty-first birthday which to keep. . . ." He realized he was shouting, and glanced fearfully around. But there wasn't a kid in sight. Nobody wanted to miss their tea and rock bun. Not even Bowdon.

She wound up her window with a small frantic hand; and drove off without a backward glance.

5

"Look at that sloppy beggar in the rear rank," said Nunk. "Handlin' himself like a fairy."

Simon surveyed the steaming block of paratroopers as they tramped past in forty-two pounds of webbing equipment. He couldn't pick out the one that looked like a fairy; they all looked very fit and tough to him. But if Nunk said so, it must be true. Nunk knew everything about soldiers. Nunk was Colonel now.

Nunk had been the man who taught Father how to parachute.

Simon had enjoyed his month; better than school. The bugles in the morning, echoing faintly over the married quarters. Bugles that meant get up to the paras; get up, get shaved, stand by your beds and get on first-works parade. While he, Simon, just lay and stretched and listened.

Following Nunk round everywhere, with the big golden labrador called Nijmegen. Nunk walking in past the guard-room, and the guard commander calling, "Guard, turn out!" All the guards moving so fast and neat, and Nunk saluting casually and saying, "Carry on, guard commander."

And the paras had watched Simon too; remembered whose son he was. Once, a small corporal had approached him, shaken hands, talked incoherently for several minutes, and fled. Later, Nunk told him that Father had rescued the corporal, wounded, under fire in Aden.

And the wide parade ground, bigger than four football pitches, that stretched to the corrugated-iron sheds where men leaped and swung in webbing harness hung from the roof. And the captive balloon, dangling its eight-hundred-foot rope with the yard-long white mark, that told the men when to open their chutes on their first descent. Oh, it was all so great. Like coming home when he was small.

"You've enjoyed your holiday?" asked Nunk. "Really?"

"Great," said Simon; but his heart sank. When people asked that, the holiday was nearly over.

"Enjoyed havin' you," said Nunk, tapping his little bamboo stick against his knife-edged trousers.

"When do I have to go?" asked Simon. He didn't want to look at Nunk; but Nunk waited in silence till he did. Nunk still looked nearly as young and handsome as a choirboy. But a choirboy with graying hair; a very tough choirboy indeed. His eyes were clear and simple as a dog's. But they had an inevitability no dog's ever had. For years and years Nunk had stood by the exit door of drop planes; looking at the paras, the young and frightened paras on their first real

39

jump, as they shuffled forward. That was where he'd got those eyes. If they wouldn't jump, Nunk pushed them, fast. If he had to, he would even put a foot in their chest and kick them out of the plane. If they had to be kicked out, Nunk didn't want to know them any more. They were sent away and Nunk forgot them. It was unbearable that Nunk should ever forget *him*.

"I'll jump," said Simon. "You won't have to push *me*."

"Good lad," said Nunk. "We'll go tomorrow. I'll take a day's leave an' run you up."

"I want to hitchhike," said Simon.

Nunk looked distinctly put out; caught at his own game of how-much-guts? But Nunk was fair; Nunk knew the rules. "O.K.," he said; but worrying like hell about what Mum would say. It was really quite funny. Simon liked teasing Nunk.

Then he thought of Joe Moreton, and the fun went away.

"This chap Moreton," said Nunk, returning his clear merciless eyes to the luckless paras, who were just pounding past again. "This chap Moreton. There's been a lot of talk since people heard he was going to marry your mother. I have to be fair, Simon, I've heard nothing bad against him. Not my sort of chap, of course—pacifist, ban-the-bomb. Got it in for us Army people of course—and the politicians. Works very hard underminin' respect for authority—too much of that these days. But his private life . . . no drugs or women or anything. Too busy knockin' authority. Met chaps like him in the old National Service days—nothing the Army did was right for them—but when it came to the crunch they did their bit. Takes all sorts. . . ."

40

"Yes," said Simon tightly. "How early can I leave?"

"Reveille. I'll book us an early call with the guard commander." But when Nunk hurried away, he didn't go toward the guardroom.

Simon sat on a fence, overlooking the village of Gorseley, Cheshire. Still early; sun not high, shadows long. The dew had searched out all the hedgerow cobwebs and decorated them with shining beads strung in unbelievable complexity. There was still a slight mist over the village, where it lay cupped in the valley around the spire of the church. Quiet; only the occasional car tore a rip in the silence, but the silence mended itself again. It would be hot, later.

He had set off at reveille. Not liking the complexity of the roads he would have to trace; the filthy black suburbs of Birmingham. Not wanting to leave the trim white railings and red firebuckets of Aldershot.

But he hadn't walked a mile before a truck had pulled up alongside. He hadn't even made a hitchhike sign. The corporal driver must have known from the haversack he was carrying that he was going somewhere. . . .

"Where you heading, mate?"

They were going to Manchester they said. To pick up some regimental silver. Wasn't it stupid, sending a three-ton truck to pick up a bit of silver? Just like the Army. . . .

Anyway, they used the motorways, driving unbelievably fast for a three-tonner, and rejoicing that they weren't held back in convoy. They offered Simon fags he refused, and chocolate that he ate, and grumbled non-stop about every officer and sergeant in the regiment. Except Nunk; which was what finally gave the game away. So Simon was not sur-

41

prised when, having reached the Holmes Chapel turnoff, where they should have dropped him, they decided to take him all the way. The Army could afford the petrol; they could fiddle the odometer to fool the QM.

But he had made them drop him at the edge of the village. He would do the last bit on his own feet; he would *not* be delivered like a parcel. Nunk would understand; Nunk liked saving his own face too. Nunk was O.K. Nunk was like Father. Father on his huge brown horse with the shining leather saddle; Father leaning down from a great height and taking him from Mum, and Mum saying be careful and Father putting the horse from a walk to a trot to a canter that jiggled Simon up and down unmercifully. Then the horse went into a gallop, and stopped jiggling and went straight and smooth and fast as a blur, and then the fence and they were flying with Father's arm very tight. And he'd thought there'd be a bump on the far side but there wasn't. And Mum running up, laughing and breathy and calling Father a bloody lunatic. . . .

Stop it, he thought, and set off walking into the village, banging his feet down hard.

Gorseley looked great from a distance, but it wasn't so hot close to. The village shop had turned itself into a mini-market, all blue-and-white stripes and freezers. There was a newly cut road on the left, offering four-bedroom executive houses. Too many new bungalows, too much white plastic fencing. Even white plastic urns. There were some old thatched cottages, but far too clean and newly painted, with aluminum up-and-over garage doors let into their sides. The village hall notice board advertised the flower show, but also a Tupperware party.

So, with the aid of Mum's precisely drawn map, he came to Mill House, with the hated white Range Rover parked in the drive. Mill House, turning a limestone gable end to the road, and stretching back deep into an orchard of ancient useless moss-grown apple trees. It had the original stone slab roof; but the chimney had been cut short by a central-heating cowl. And back among the trees he could see a non-sense of all glass windows on the first floor above a two-car garage. The gravel drive was far too beautifully raked. Joe Moreton had too much money and no sense of how things were done.

He knocked. No answer; only somewhere a little rush of water, so somebody was up. He knocked again. Then tried the door. It opened, and he went in.

Dim. The deep slow tick of a grandfather clock. Drawn curtains. On the hall mantelpiece, a brass Buddha; no, three brass Buddhas. And a huge one on a table at the foot of the stair. Everywhere, Buddhas. Tiny ones two inches tall; the biggest nearly three feet.

It wasn't a house, it was a rotten museum. And a funny musky smell. Marijuana? No, Nunk had said no drugs.

He called out hallo. Nobody answered. But there were noises somewhere. He advanced again, trailing his haver-sack along the thick carpet and up the stairs.

"You're *fat!*" Jane's voice, all gloaty. He could tell she was pinching rolls of someone's bare flesh. Jane's "you're fat" game was played at every opportunity. His own stom-ach tingled at the memory. He nearly laughed. Some things hadn't changed. . . .

"You're so fat—look!" She giggled. "An' look at all the hairs on your chest. You're like a big fat *monkey*. An' . . .

there's hairs under your arms an' hairs inside your nose an' hairs on the end of your nose. No one should have hairs on the end of their nose. I'm going to pull them *out!*"

Screams of high-pitched glee. "Don't do that—you'll bump me off. Don't blow up your belly like a *horse*."

Simon stood so still, he might have been frozen into ice. Only, he let go the strap of the haversack and it fell silently onto the thick, thick carpet of the upstairs corridor.

Jane changed tack. She was only ever cruel for a bit; pinching, or trying to pick away a bit of skin with her fingernail over and over again, or twisting ears. Then she got worried.

"I love you. Do-you-love-me?"

Deep rumble. Rumbling laugh. Faint smell of man drifting down the passage, mixed with a hint of Mum's perfume.

"You-must-love-me-Joe.   Or-I'll-pull-every-one-of-your-hairs-out-an'-then-you'll-be-all-bald-like-an-egg."

"O.K. I love you. I surrender."

"Just as well, my dear. Now bump me up and down again."

A soft movement of cloth on cloth took Simon's unfocused eyes to the end of the corridor. Mum was standing there in a long turquoise dressing gown that stretched to her feet, tea tray in her hand. Her hair was scraped back with a comb, early morning. Her face sleepy and shockingly gentle.

"Simon?" she said, puzzled, as if he was a ghost. She kept peering at him; his face must be in shadow or something. "Simon? Simon, we weren't expecting you till lunch. Nunk said. . . ."

She advanced, swishing softly.

"Simon, what are you standing there like that for, you

44

silly goose? You gave me quite a turn. Cat got your tongue? It's just that when Nunk phoned. . . ."

She got near enough to see his face. Her blue eyes, which had been so wide they were almost black, suddenly narrowed to pinpoints. Horseshoe-shaped anxiety lines hooked round the corners of her mouth.

"*Simon!* What's the *matter?*"

She let go the tray with both hands, and it crashed, sending out stars of milk and tea across the carpet. One hand went to her mouth.

"Simon, what are you looking like that for?"

Looking like what? He didn't *know* how he looked. The look on his face stood like a monster between them. *He* couldn't control the look on his face. *He* didn't know how to work the muscles. But he knew what the look must look like, because he could see its reflection on her face. He turned in terror and ran out of the house. And not all her calling would fetch him back.

The devils had returned.

6

HE RAN OUT THROUGH the gate, turned left, ran a hundred yards and ducked back through a gap in the hedge. He didn't want her to find him. He heard her voice approaching, calling. She must look very silly, wandering up the road in her dressing gown. She got pretty near; too near. Then her voice lost hope and dwindled.

Then he remembered he'd left his haversack lying on the hall floor and that made him feel lonely. It hadn't held much: Mum's map, a few sandwiches that Auntie Marge had made, a plastic map and Father's army badge. But now he had nothing.

For the first time he looked around. Saw the roof of Mill House over the apple trees, too close for comfort, and slipped deeper into the hedge. For the rest, he could see nothing but turnips; a field of turnips growing in neat geometric rows as far as the eye could see. Their geometry only broken by pale random fringes of weed. The turnips were in full leaf, purply blue gray, full of darker blue shadows. The wind, coming across them, lifted their undersides in silvery waves. They whispered together like friends. Somehow, he felt they were happy. The smell of turnip soothed him.

He'd never seen a bigger field. There were dips in the ground, where hedgerows had been rooted out to make several fields into one. The great field rose slightly, then fell gently away. The turnips got smaller and smaller and tinier and tinier, until looking at them did funny things to your eyes.

At that point he saw a roof, just sticking up over the faint far edge of the field. Screwing up his eyes against the sun, he could see the roof was very like Mill House. Huge simple stone slabs. Somehow, it looked . . . inviting.

Don't be silly, he told himself. How can a roof be *inviting?* There'll be people living there. They'll stare at me. If I knock they'll want to know what I want. . . . Angrily, he turned his eyes away. But there was nothing else to look at but the hedge and the turnips. Soon his eyes returned to that roof again. There was one chimney, but no smoke coming from it. Why *should* there be smoke coming from it, in the middle of summer?

46

Then he saw there was a slab missing from the roof, just at the base of the chimney. And he knew, looking at the black hole the missing slab had left, that the place was empty. Inviting . . . inviting. . . . A quivery, illogical excitement filled him. He thought of burglary. He thought, absurdly, of Goldilocks and the Three Bears. . . .

Well, he had to do something, go somewhere. He couldn't just stand in the hedge all day, till Mum got organized and found him, and thought him a baby, hanging round waiting to be found.

He'd have to walk all the way round the hedge to get to the roof. If he tried crossing the open field, they'd see him. He walked. Difficult. Some places he had to crawl under the hedge; even at one point into a ditch full of long grass and cobwebs full of dead insects that stuck to his face. Sometimes the hedge thrust out wide branches, forcing him out among the deep sandy furrows of the field, where his feet slipped and ripped wet skin off the turnips, increasing their smell. He kept getting pricked, and began to sweat. He took off his anorak and tied it round his waist. But it kept getting caught; and once, thrusting forward in a temper, he tore it. That upset him. The anorak was practically all he had left in the world. If he wasn't careful, he'd end up with nothing.

Finally, he decided going round the hedge would take all day. He must go straight across. Mill House was far off, now; the inviting roof nearer. He'd step carefully, so as not to harm the turnips.

He hadn't gone ten yards when a voice called, "Boy!" making him jump a yard in the air.

But it was nobody he knew. It was a vicar, peering

47

through a gap in the hedge, from astride a bicycle with a basket on the front. The vicar wore a pale gray linen coat and straw hat, the kind old men wear. He did not look particularly old; the few strands of his hair that showed were still dark and wavy. But he looked lifeless, as if he could never have laughed for the last forty years. There was an air about him that would stop you laughing anywhere near him. Yet though his brow was heavily wrinkled, he did not look particularly miserable. As if it was his job to stop people laughing, and he was good at it and rather enjoyed it.

"Boy!"

He went back reluctantly; the vicar had a voice like the masters at school.

"Boy, what are you doing? That is not *your* field. Those are not *your* turnips."

"I was being careful."

"That is not enough. Can you guarantee that your foot will not slip once *all* the way across? That you will not harm *one* turnip?"

Simon could only shake his head.

"Then you are betraying a trust. That farmer bought his turnip seeds with his own money, which he earned with the sweat of his brow. He planted them with the sweat of his brow, and left them to grow, trusting all men that they would not harm them."

For God's sake, thought Simon. What's one or two broken turnip leaves? The farmer probably couldn't give two monkeys. He mustn't know how many he's got. Nor care. He probably expects hundreds to be stolen or eaten by rabbits. You silly old goat. . . .

48

"Oh, you may say," continued the clergyman, "what does one leaf or one turnip or even a hundred turnips matter? But it does. If you destroy one leaf, can you remake it? The world is *changed*. *You* are changed, in a way you cannot know. Never a sparrow falls to the ground but is seen by your Father. . . ."

He's nuts, thought Simon. But on careful inspection, the vicar didn't look alive enough to be a dangerous nut. Not the sort that gives sweets to children. Just the sort who spends all day watching a turnip field, counting the leaves.

"Now go your way in peace," said the vicar. "Be thankful you have been stopped in time. God be with you." And he pedaled away. He could have been a gray ghost, except that the cranks of his bicycle groaned for lack of oil.

Perhaps your God cares about poor unoiled crank shafts too, thought Simon. But he didn't try to cross the field again; he knew the vicar's sort: the sort that would try to catch you out a second time, and would hang around all day to do it.

Wearily he began to work his way round the hedge again. Occasionally, he cast longing glances across at Mill House; not thinking about Joe Moreton, but about glasses of orange squash with ice, and a breakfast of bacon and eggs. But the other roof was close, now, and the hole in it summoned him like a dark unblinking eye.

He came to the great pond first; desperately thirsty. But the water wasn't the kind you could drink. It lay at the bottom of a stone wall, six feet below Simon's shoes. If you fell in, you could never climb out again. And the water was dark gray, as though somebody had mixed soot with it. Yet you could see down through it, in the bright sun shine, to dim beds of weed that had gray scum growing on them. The only cheerful thing was masses of tiny bright-green leaves floating on the surface, almost a mad yellow in the sun. But they only made the pond seem deeper, darker, dirtier.

Further out were lily pads—not well organized, but a wreck, a jumble of leaf points sticking up like the bows of sunken ships. Further out again, a densely wooded island. Two brown ducks swam round the island as Simon watched. Normally, ducks cheered him; fat, quacky and bright. But these looked furtive, as if they knew they shouldn't be there. They soon vanished, bigger one in front.

Simon walked along the massive wall, toward the strange roof. Funny, the roof came right down to the pond wall. Must be a *very* low building. . . . But as he reached it, he gasped. The ground suddenly dropped twenty feet. He was no longer standing on a wall, but on top of a dam. And the roof belonged to a water mill, built against the dam. There was a huge water wheel, red with rust. He ran down red stone steps into the garden in front of the mill.

Only it was no longer a garden. It was a jungle. Rose trees extended long thin branches like bending fishing rods, ten feet in the air. Laden with tiny white roses. The branches looked unsafe; waved wildly with every breath of air. There were poor grey lupins too, desperately struggling not to drown in the engulfing sea of grass. Most of the grass was dead and rotting. Dead grass thrust up through dead grass, with the living grass just managing to push out of the top, a flicker of green.

There was no pathway from the foot of the red steps, except the low tunnels wild things make. Nobody had come this way for a long, long time.

Dead grass had grown halfway up the front door; a front door that didn't really go with the rest of the mill. Modernish and painted a sun-blistered maroon, with two pebble-glass panels at the top. One panel was neatly broken, just above the lock. Not vandals. Somebody had broken the glass to get in; somebody who didn't want to do more damage than he had to. . . . The door opened inward, but jammed halfway. Simon squeezed past.

He was in a dim, whitewashed living room. Though the fireplace was only a black hole in the whitewashed wall, with rusty bars across to keep the coals from falling out, there was still ash in the grate. A bed stood in one corner, under the window. Just a brown mattress, with a pile of brown blankets neatly folded. Too neatly folded; folded by somebody who didn't fold blankets every day. A wooden table, with a wooden chair pushed back from it. On the table, a stump of candle in a tobacco tin, Swan Vestas matches, a well-bitten pipe and a newspaper.

Simon began to back out in embarrassment. This *was* somebody's home. They might be back any moment. He remembered again the story of the Three Bears, and giggled. Who's been sleeping in *my* bed? Then, abruptly, he stopped giggling. Somebody might be listening, beyond that far door. . . .

But the newspaper on the table drew him irresistibly; a *Daily Mail*. But surely the *Mail* was smaller than that these days.

The headline said:

STALINGRAD ARMY WIPED OUT

The date was Monday, February 1, 1943.

He grabbed it, and it crumbled to brown flakes under his hand.

51

He stared round the dim room, wrinkling up his eyes in bafflement. 1943? But he *knew* somebody had just left the room. You could always tell when people had. You could feel their presence still. At home, when he found the house empty, he could always tell if Mum had just popped out, or been gone for hours.

Then he knew somebody was watching him; from the left. He froze, between embarrassment and terror. He could not move his legs; only turn his head, straining to see out of the corner of his eye.

There were three people, standing in the darkest place, watching him. They did not move either.

A big broad man—a woman—a smaller man. . . .

Then he laughed, shrilly. Because they were just old coats, hanging on pegs.

He walked across and poked their flat damp emptiness. A dark blue raincoat—a gray tweed woman's coat—a brown overall like ironmongers sometimes wore. And above them, completing the illusion of people, three hats hung: a rolled balaclava helmet, a brown felt woman's hat and a check cap.

Three different people, because the coats were all different sizes. A big man, a smallish woman and a smallish man, but broad. He knew this because he suddenly had the irresistible impulse to try the coats on. Took them down off the wall, one after the other, careful not to tear them. Paraded up and down the room in them, though his skin crawled at their heavy mustiness. He even wore the hats as well, though their dampness made his scalp prickle. He giggled again; who's been trying on *my* coat? He had never known himself act so silly. It must be the heat, and no breakfast.

The woman's and the small man's coats were just a little too long for him; but the big man's coat slithered along the dusty floor behind him as he walked. He hung everything back on the pegs, careful to put the right coat under the right hat, suddenly feeling he'd been terribly cheeky.

But the inhabitants of the mill didn't seem to mind. In fact the room seemed to get friendlier, homelier. He sat on the wooden chair, feeling weary. Fell into a daydream. They must be—must have been a wartime family . . . the miller's family . . . mother, father and son. Going through the Battle of Britain together—only there hadn't been much of a Battle of Britain in Cheshire. Now if this had been Kent. . . .

The big man in the blue coat would be the father, busy milling . . . the son would help him. The mother cooking bread from their own flour . . . at least millers* wouldn't have gone hungry in the war . . . setting snares for rabbits . . . he could almost smell new bread and rabbit stew—he liked new bread and rabbit stew. Cosy . . . a mum who stayed home and was always there when you needed her; a father around who you could help and ask questions.

Tears pricked his eyes and he dashed them furiously away.

Suppose the father had been killed in the war? But no— somehow from the coat you could tell he'd been big and fat, too old for a soldier. And all the coats looked equally ancient. Wherever the family had gone, they had left together on the 1st of February, 1943. Thirty-two years ago; a long, long time. He came out of his dream and remembered the grass growing up the front door, and the pathless garden.

And who had broken the pane of glass in the door? Burglars? But it didn't look as if they'd stolen anything, done any harm. Just folded up those blankets in that cold, unnatural way. Burglars wouldn't bother to fold blankets. . . .

He suddenly felt intensely protective about the mill and the family. And felt, in a funny way, the room respond. Nothing spooky; not spooky at all. It was just you could tell if a place or people liked you or not. Simon could always tell when he was wanted.

But if three people lived here—had lived here—why only one single bed? He got up and opened the door that must lead into the mill.

Darkness, and a cold, cold smell; damp earth and slimy water and rotting plants: a graveyard smell. A draught came out of the dark, and went past him as he stood in the doorway. It stirred his hair and cooled all the sweat on his body. Every nerve said run, *run.*

But Woods did not run; Woods headed straight for what they were afraid of. He braced himself against the fear, as if it were a wave of the sea, and when it passed, he stepped out gingerly into the dark.

It wasn't totally dark. As his eyes adjusted, he could see several rows of faint blue horizontal slits, set into the walls. And the blue light bounded round, picking out corners of great wooden wheels and axles. Only the mill machinery; nothing to be afraid of.

Then he saw the blond man hanging; from a rope around his neck. Legs dangling, body swaying gently in the breeze that came out of the dark and passed through the door behind Simon. Simon felt his whole body go rigid; felt his

54

knuckles go to his mouth; felt his teeth bite on them, bottling up a scream.

Woods did not run. Father, he thought, and walked toward the hanged man.

Touched him.

And the moment he touched, everything changed shape. It was far too light to be a hanged man.

A sack. Thirty-two years ago, the miller had hauled a sack of grain up on a hoist, and left it hanging, that last day. Over the years the sack had dampened, rotted, burst, spilling the grain on the floor. Now the burst bottom of the sack dangled down in rags, making the hanged man's legs. And over the years, the rope had chafed half-through; two pale strands of frayed hemp hung loose, making the hanged man's hair. And animals had come and eaten the grain lying beneath, leaving only a clotted black mess.

So simple. . . . But he still ran back into the living room and slammed the door on the mill; he wasn't interested in the workings of the mill, he told himself.

With the door shut, the living room closed round him, friendlier than ever. How light it seemed, how warm and dry on his skin. Simon went all floppy and giggly again. What's wrong with me today?

Nothing, said the living room; silly boy. Nothing to be afraid of in an old sack. He smiled and mooched lazily around. The Swan Vestas wouldn't light; in fact the box fell apart in his hand. He felt bad about that, even if it had really been caused by the damp. He put the matchbox together again, and put it back on the table exactly where it had been, in the rectangular mark in the dust. It looked O.K. if you didn't touch it. He didn't want the family upset when they came back. Could they come back, after thirty years? Well, the son might. . . .

He mooched further, but there wasn't much else. Just a piece of folded brownish paper under the bed. Someone had put a cluddering great foot on it, stamping it into a narrow dart.

He unfolded it. It was a page torn from a report book: *Cheshire Constabulary*. The police must have come after whoever broke in. But all it said was "On Monday morning, the 1st of Febuary." Then someone had realized they'd spelled "February" wrong, crossed it out and torn the page out of the book. The only odd thing was that the writing was a bit shaky; and blurred, as if something had been spilled on it. Simon smelled the stain. It smelled, very faintly, like sick; but after thirty years perhaps anything smelled like sick.

A movement at the outside door made him jump. But it was only a large ginger-and-white cat peering in. He liked cats. He called, "Puss-puss-puss," but it stayed outside the door, meowing a terrible complaint the way some cats do. So he had to go to it. It scampered away a few feet into the ruined garden, then fell into a limp. Something was wrong with its left forefoot. And it made no attempt to struggle, as he picked it up.

He got another shock, then. It had looked so big and strong and clean, but it weighed no more than a feather. He could feel all the big bones under its too-loose bag of skin. He knew farm cats were lean, but. . . . And it had two rows of big funny bumps along its belly.

Suddenly he knew four things. It was a she cat, and wild—lived by hunting. She was hurt, so she couldn't hunt.

And somewhere she had kittens. Were they starving too?

He must get food, quick. Shops? He had enough money for cat food, but not enough for cat food and can-opener, and a pint of milk and to feed himself. And if he was not quick, she might be gone by the time he got back.

Mum. Mum would help. He couldn't stand that rotten centrally heated Buddha museum; but he didn't hate it enough to let kittens die. And kittens were more important than rotten old turnip leaves. He ran straight across the turnip field. Maybe the vicar *would* see him, but if he ran straight for Mill House, Mum would deal with the vicar.

7

THERE WAS A GREEN GATE in the hedge between turnip field and Mill House. He hung on it, panting, and just then Mum came out of the house. With her into-battle look on her face. Chin stuck out, wearing trousers and anorak.

"Mum?"

She whirled. Her eyes flamed blue. "Where the hell . . . ?"

He found the handle and went through the gate. "Mum, there's a cat. She's hurt . . . she's starving . . . there's kittens."

She took one look at his face, and postponed the telling off. Later he'd cop it. But Mum always put first things first.

He followed her into the kitchen. She swept round the shelves like a tornado, yelling questions over her shoulder. Snatched a stainless steel dish, two cans of stewing steak, a can opener from a drawer, a bottle of milk from the fridge, a rug from a chair, the first-aid kit from the top of the cupboard. All into a duffle bag that was hanging on the door.

"I'll just leave a note for Joe." She reached for the scribble pad that hung over the sink.

"There's not time!" he yelled, suddenly jealous.

"Joe's out looking for you. I don't want him going frantic about me as well. Won't be a tick." She scrawled "Simon back. Gone help hurt cat in mill across back field. Luv. Deb." Left it lying on the table and headed across the field, leaving the gate open. She strode straight across the rows of turnips without even bothering to look, leaving a bruised and battered trail and even kicking the odd unfortunate leaf high in the air. Simon wondered what the vicar would say. If, with Mum, he dared say anything.

But Mum was making so much noise she'd scare the cat. . . .

Then she stopped on top of the mill dam and opened the can of steak. She gave it to him in the dish. "You go ahead, Simon. The cat knows you. Give me a call when you're ready. I'll wait here." She looked down at the pond. "Yuk!" She lit a fag, screwing her eyes up, and threw the dead match into the water.

He went down very quietly. Stopped by the still-open maroon door and called, "Puss-puss-puss." No answer. He called again. Still no answer. He went on calling, despair growing in his heart; staring down at the suddenly useless mound of steak. A big fat fly settled on it. He brushed it off with a gesture of rage, close to tears.

Then, suddenly, the cat was round his feet; rubbing against his legs. He knelt and gave her the dish. She sniffed

cautiously, then fell to eating with a fearsome silent deter-
mination, ploughing her nose through the brown heap,
swallowing in huge gulps. All her long hunger in her eating.

He tiptoed away up the steps and signaled Mum, not
wanting to shout for fear of scaring the cat. Mum was
crouched on the dam wall, staring at the water; but she
saw his wave straight away. Together, they watched the
cat lick the stainless steel dish back to spotlessness.

"Give her the other can," said Simon. "She's still
hungry."

"No. It would kill her. She has to get used to eating
again." Mum stroked the cat's back gently, aghast at the
knobs on its spine. "You saved her just in time, Simon. I
wonder if we can have a look at her foot? Do you think
she'll let us?"

The cat had begun to wash her face.

"I think so," said Simon. "It looks pretty swollen. Shall
we take her to the vet? What about the kittens?"

Just then came a loud continuous noise from the dam
wall above. An all-too-familiar noise. Jane doing her baby
act. "Ooh, look, Joe. It's like a *jungle. A real* jungle. You
be a nellephant, Joe. You're the nellephant and I can ride
on your back an' we can go shooting tigers. The cat can
be the tiger. But you're big an' strong. You're not afraid
of tigers, are you, Joe?"

The cat looked up in alarm. Simon grabbed for her,
but she was gone with painful leaps into the depths of the
long grass.

"Shit!" said Simon, looking up at the dam wall with hate.

"She's only little, Simon."

"She ought to have more *sense*."

59

Joe clumped down the steps with ponderous care, Jane on his back. She was waving a frond of cow parsley with one hand, and clutching Joe round the head with the other. The remains of Joe's hair was standing up like a pathetic bush. His blue shirt, open to his hairy navel, was dark and wet under both arms; he was sweating like a big fat pig, and his paunch hung out. Jane let go of his head, and swung the cow parsley at Simon with both hands.

"There's the tiger, Joe. Bang! He's *dead*. Good nellephant." She shot Mum too, for good measure. The pair of them looked bloody ridiculous.

Joe put Jane down. She dug her fingers hard into his shoulder; but he didn't flinch. He straightened up, brushed his hair back into place, looked at Mum and said, "What goes, then?"

"We got a can of steak down her. I think she's gone to feed her kittens."

"You scared her off," said Simon, looking at nobody. "You scared her off, making all that stupid noise. You should have *known*. . . ." He nearly added "You big fat ape," but Mum said, *"Simon!"* warningly.

"Oh, she'll come back," said Joe. "Now she knows where the food is. She won't snuff it overnight, not with a can of steak inside her."

"Her foot's hurt," shouted Simon, at the mill door if anywhere. "It's swollen. It's probably septic. She might get gangrene. She might lose her foot. She might *die*."

"We've done all we can for now," said Mum, with determined lightness.

"This is a curious building," said Joe, sounding as real as a three-pound note. "I'd noticed the roof, but I'd no

60

idea what it was . . . interesting. A water mill—"

"No—it's a yogurt factory, actually."

"Simon! One more word . . . *one* more word!"

Simon shrugged, still staring at the mill door.

"Must have a look at this," said Joe. Like he owned the bloody mill too. He forced back the door with clumsy shoves and went in.

"Oooh, Joe, isn't it *creepy*. I'm *scared*." Jane was back in his arms again, loving every minute of it.

Joe looked round, eyes suddenly sharp. Seemed to be listening. In that mood, he looked different. You had to admit it. Like a dog that sees a rabbit. Suddenly you didn't notice his yobbish flab. He frowned; then actually shivered. "I don't care for this place much. Odd vibes. . . ."

"Just an old mill," said Simon. Glad that Joe was scared of it. Yellow ban-the-bomb pacifist. Pacifists were scared of everything. That's why they were pacifists. No guts.

"I don't like it either," said Mum.

Joe picked at the newspaper on the table. But it just fell into tinier and tinier bits, crumbling under his big sausage fingers. Simon didn't enlighten him. He laughed when Joe picked up the Swan Vestas box and it fell apart again. It was Joe's fault now.

Joe opened the door into the mill proper and they all followed silently, hesitantly; Simon last. The same cold smell, the same draught; and darkness—until Joe forced open one of the slatted windows, letting in light and a gust of warm air. Now you could see that the mill was just one huge room, three stories high. No ceiling, just rafters and the underside of roofing flags, cemented with rough blobs to keep out the wind. The rafters were hung with looping drapes of cobweb, that billowed like silk curtains in the sudden breeze.

Inside that dim cavern had been built a whole hamster cage of heavy wood. Huge vertical posts a foot thick; white-washed, but the whitewash had flaked off and the flakes hung trapped in more cobwebs, spinning wildly now. The posts had been eaten into; small holes of woodworm, bigger holes of death watch beetle; gnaw marks where something bigger still had been at them, a squirrel or a rat perhaps. Between the vertical posts were platforms and staircases and handrails. Huge wooden wheels stood vertical and horizontal, like the works of a giant clock, cogs still black with grease. And loops of rope and gray canvas drive belts soared up to the ceiling, like in a church belfry or sailing ship.

Nervously, they trooped upward. Each tread of the staircases was worn down to a knife blade by the passing of feet. But only on one side; the other side of each tread was good and square. The treads were worn alternately on the left and right. Simon could imagine the miller nipping round his wooden cage, practised as a hamster; always putting the same foot on the same stair: left, right, left, right. It made Simon feel very close to the miller; as if *he* was the miller, working his mill. The miller must have known every inch of the mill; so well that he could work it in the dark. The handrails were chalky, with worn holes, but their edges and ends were rounded and blackly greasy, from the palms of the miller's hands.

There were other signs of the miller, too; in one corner, a face mask against flour dust hung on a rusty nail, and a long brown apron with a loop of binder twine on top to

62

hold it round the miller's neck. An old wicker chair, with
on oilskin cape slung on it; nearby on a beam, a rusted
ashtray full of fag ends. That was where the miller would
have taken his break. Joe tried to lift the oilskin, but it
was stuck too close to the wicker; the marks of the wicker
had pressed through. When Joe heaved, the oilskin tore.

Clumsy elephant, thought Simon How *dare* you? It
doesn't belong to you; it belongs to the miller.

There was a soft creaking suddenly behind them, that
made them all turn. But it was only the old grain sack,
suspended over a trapdoor and swinging in the new draught
the opening of the window had made. The blond strand
of hemp fluttered limply and the canvas legs danced.

"The trapdoor opens upward only," said Joe Elephant
Clever-cuts. "It's for hauling sacks up." He went and stood
on the trapdoor, which didn't give way, even under his
great weight.

"How did they get sacks down then, big-head?" asked
Simon.

"Didn't have to," said Joe smugly. "The grain came up
in sacks and went down through the grindstones and
emerged at the bottom as flour." He pointed down through
the open hamster cage to where, on the ground floor, two
chutes stood, one marked BRAN and the other FLOUR.

They wandered down again. There were signs of the
miller everywhere; hanks of binder twine hung on nails,
ready to tie the mouths of sacks; little rows of penciled
marks on the wall; four vertical strokes with a diagonal
across, meaning five; five bags ground today. They walked
on narrow gangways over pits of green darkness, where
wheels glinted. Down to the bottom cellar with its acid-

sweet smell of bare damp soil; where a sack of grain had rotted and sprouted, and then withered and died. Where there was a row of spare wheels; whitewashed, but the rust had spread over it like a rash of red pimples.

"Ugh!" said Mum. "Give me sunlight. Let's go home."

"It's an amazing place," said Joe. "Wonderfully preserved."

"I wonder if it still works," said Simon dreamily. "I wonder how you start it up."

Joe caught him by the shoulder, roughly. Simon pulled back out of his grip with even more violence, making Joe say, "Sorry. But I'd better warn you now. I may not be much of a countryman, but I do know about water mills. They are *very* frail things, even when they're in working order."

"Frail?" sneered Simon, looking at the foot-thick timbers.

"Don't underestimate the power of water," said Joe solemnly. "It's possible even with a working mill to race it to pieces if you open the sluice too wide and let too much water in. This mill may look perfect, but it can't have been used in years. Timbers eaten away, axles gone dry, wheels rusted. If you tried to start this mill without six months' restoration, it could explode like a bomb." His stupid face was owlish with concern.

"Don't get your knickers in a twist," said Simon.

Mum sighed loudly, in a way that meant storm warnings.

Outside, they looked for the cat, but she was nowhere to be seen. As they headed back across the turnip field, following the now all-too-visible trail, Mum said:

"It's weird. That marvelous old place just being allowed

to rot. The National Trust should take it over . . . there can't be that many left."

Joe stopped. "Funny. I've just remembered, when I was a little kid, the bigger lads would dare each other to go up to the mill and touch the door and run away again. I told my mother and she nearly went mad; got out her big black Bible and made me swear on it never to go *near* the mill. I can never remember her getting so upset; all white and chewing her lips. She scared me silly. But I was only a toddler—I didn't even know where the mill was. For me, then, going to the village shop was like crossing the Sahara. And later I forgot. Well, now I've finally been there . . . but I doubt I shall go again."

And out in the mid-day sun, in the middle of the great field of turnips, Joe shivered again.

Simon turned away, to hide the sneer on his face.

8

AS SOON AS SIMON FINISHED breakfast, he set off back to the mill. Carrying the duffle bag that hadn't been unpacked since yesterday. It was O.K. The rug inside was from their old home; and Mum's first-aid kit. And a can opener was just a can opener; and a can of meat was just a can of meat, and a bottle of milk was just a bottle of milk.

Nothing belonged to Joe Moreton.

He went straight across the turnip field. Damn the vicar. He wasn't about anyway. Probably down in Knutsford, lecturing kids that if they dropped a lollypop stick in the road they would change Eternity.

The clouds were low and heavy today; he thought he felt a spot of rain. It set him worrying about the cat. Would she come back if it rained? Were the kittens in a dry spot? He quickened his pace.

But he needn't have worried. She came running as soon as he descended the red steps. Hovered, watching his hands, bad paw held in the air in her anxiety for food. He wondered suddenly if she had been the miller's cat. No, stupid. Cats only lived about sixteen years. . . . But she might be a descendant of the miller's cat. A great-great-great-great-great-granddaughter. Cats bred a new generation every year; thirty-two generations . . . not far short of a thousand years in human terms . . . only sixty-five human generations back to Jesus Christ.

As he was thinking that, the rain came. Solid rods, slashing cruelly at the grass in the garden; making the long wild branches of the rose trees sag and swing alarmingly. He ran for the door, and left it open for the cat to follow.

"Puss, puss, puss."

He got the can of steak out on the table, and opened it, expecting any moment to feel the cat rub against his legs. She didn't. He looked up, dish of food in hand. She was peering round the open door, but she wouldn't come in.

"Come on, you silly puss." He went to grab her, but she backed away into the garden. Already she was soaking, wretched.

He went out and grabbed her. She came to his arms willingly enough, even purring. But when he tried to carry her inside, she went mad. He tried to hold her, but she flailed out with her claws, narrowly missing his eye in her panic. Finally, with a convulsive spring of unbelievable

66

strength, she leaped over his shoulder and was free. She retreated a few yards; her fur was sleeked with wet now, making her look like a tatty walking skeleton. He rubbed blood off his cheek with the sleeve of his anorak.

"You *stupid* cat."

She raised her hurt paw again, and cried piteously for the food.

"All right!" he shouted, and put the dish just inside the open door. Her nose twitched as she scented it. She came eagerly, then stopped right on the threshold. And would not cross it. He pushed the dish nearer; only half an inch inside. She tried to reach across and dab it with her swollen paw, but even the paw would not cross the invisible point where the door usually was. As if there were a pane of glass there, and she meowing on the other side, like a cat he had once seen locked inside a shop window over a weekend. The rain was dripping off her now. He had never seen a cat in such a mess. In her weakened state she would catch pneumonia.

"Oh, all *right*." He pushed the dish outside so violently, it tipped off the step and spilled onto the trampled grass. She fell on it as ravenously as a wolf. The rain belted bare spots of pink skin through her fur, but she never even seemed to notice. As she finished, he poured the cream off the milk among the last traces of meat in the dish, making a brown, coffee-like mixture. She scoffed the lot. When his milk bottle was half-empty, she left as suddenly as she'd come; but he noted carefully which way she went, from the waving of the grass. Round the far corner of the mill. . . . When the rain stopped, he would go and find the nest where she had her kittens.

Meanwhile. . . .

The mill was exactly the same. The box of Swan Vestas that Joe Moreton had spilled still lay on the table. Joe Moreton was afraid of the mill; Joe Moreton had said he wouldn't come here again.

Good. The mill was all his now.

He looked at the coats in the corner. Had they moved in the semi-darkness, seemed to nod agreement? Or had they just swayed in the endless draughts?

All right, he said, nodding at the coats. The mill is *ours* now. Then he shook himself, as if he'd been silly. . . . But if Joe Moreton had his rotten Buddha museum, the mill was bigger, grander. Full of new sounds; patter of rain on the stone slab roof, far away. Tiny gurgle of water from the water spouts like faceless gargoyles, high up in the walls. Somewhere in the main part of the mill a window was banging in the rain wind. The window that Joe Moreton had opened as if he owned the place; then left open carelessly. Simon went through the door to shut it.

Yesterday's footprints lay clear in the flour-like dust. His own, with ribbed soles; Mum's pointed ones; Jane's little ones; Joe Moreton's elephantine ones. He walked round wiping out Joe's footprints with a twist of his foot, wherever he could find them.

The vertical main drive shaft caught his eye, with the great grinding millstone at the bottom. An octagonal oak pillar, with a huge wooden cog fastened horizontally across the top. Struts went up from the shaft to support the cog; diagonally, like the diagonal strut on a gallows. But he was far more interested in the way the cog fitted into the next cog, which fitted into the next shaft, which had another cog. . . . He began to understand how the mill worked. Understanding, he climbed slowly upward to the very top platform.

There, he found a big wooden lever; whitewashed below, but rounded and black above, with the grease of the miller's hand. He put his hand to it; it fitted his hand so perfectly, like a sword he'd once picked up in the Tower of London and been told off for. Something made him pull the lever gently toward him. It seemed the thing to do, somehow.

There came a faint sour-sweet smell: the smell of rain hitting dry summer dust; a smell he'd always loved. It came from a long wooden trough running past him. As he looked, the floor of the trough changed from rough wood to shining blackness.

Water was running into the mill. All over, different sounds of rushing waters, like little waterfalls.

Then the noise of a dustbin being rolled by bin men, right beneath his feet. A dustbin two inches thick. . . .

Then *tong . . . tong tong tong tong tong*—a noise like a boy rattling an iron bar along iron railings.

The whole mill began to vibrate gently up through the soles of his training shoes.

Entranced, he moved about. The sounds changed as he moved. Went deeper. Roaring, like a lion, chained up underground. Water going *shee-shee-shee,* like a heart beating. Rumbles like indigestion inside his own body, so deep down were they. Again, *shee-shee-shee,* like the blood pounding in his his own ears.

But the mill didn't run evenly, like a vacuum cleaner. It varied like a living thing. In the long wooden trough, the water surged deep for a few seconds, then shallow again. The machinery would run quietly for a while, then break out with a violent chatter of gears. Even the quiet-and-loud patches were never quite the same length. You could never get *used* to them; you had to listen carefully for every change, because it was new.

You could go on listening forever. He wandered slowly down the narrow stairs and gangways, over the throbbing pits. It *was* like being inside a clock. Segments of wheels turning in the gray light from the still-open window; then spinning off into pitch darkness. The thick grease on the cogwheels was like blue black butter.

The inside of a great drum, with a dozen drummers playing, loud and soft, near and far. But the biggest drummer was still lower, beneath his feet.

Down, down, he went. To where the brick of the walls sweated. And the white roots of plants pushed down through the brick arch overhead; tried vainly to curl back up, back into the brick from whence they came; but they never would, they'd just hang helpless forever in the dark. The only homely thing was the lettering on the bricks, which said the name of a firm in Manchester.

He was near now. Near to the biggest drummer. And then, in the last ghost of light, he saw it: the huge water wheel, red-leaded turning in its tomb of black stone, turning, turning slowly; leaking water like a rainstorm, sometimes throwing down whole sheets. The metal of the axle, inside the huge rumbling noise, whimpered like a small hurt animal; or chirruped like a canary. The wheel was barnacled with rust, like a rock at low tide.

All these sounds the miller must have known; been

70

deafened by for years. Or did he get so used to them that he could still pick out the softest footfall behind him . . . ?

Simon whirled in terror.

There was nothing there. But he knew that if there had been a footstep, *he* wouldn't have heard it. Soaked with sweat and spray, he ran, and did not stop running till he was again on the topmost platform, panting. He pushed the starting lever back the way it had come.

Nothing happened. Inexorably the mill ground on. He pushed the lever harder. But dared not push too hard, because there were worm holes in the whitewashed wood, and if the lever snapped he could *never* stop the mill and its terrible sound would pursue him right across the turnip field and into Mill House and then . . . something awful would happen.

But the mill was growing quieter. Dying, dying, dying. He waited with his fingers crossed until the last rattle died away.

It was utterly silent; even the rain had stopped.

Then he thought about the cat, and his body relaxed into a state of . . . everydayness. He made his way downstairs, shut the slatted window and began picking his way through the garden. The long vegetation soaked through his anorak; drenched him to the waist so his trousers rubbed the inside of his legs. But he didn't mind; that was part of everydayness too.

When he got there, the cat's nest was surprisingly obvious. A brick coalshed built .against the massive red stone wall of the mill, round the corner. On the low heap of coal was a collapsed cardboard box marked, barely discernibly: *Dried Egg, 36 cans. Produce of U.S.A.* Inside the box was a mixture of hay and torn-up newspaper. On top, the cat lay with her kittens, who were sucking at her furiously, pushing each other away with a savage paddling of tiny perfect paws. Only they were thin, dreadfully thin, like their mother. So thin that even Simon, who'd handled plenty of kittens, couldn't guess how old they were. Kittens should have fat tums that felt like tennis balls. These didn't.

Three kittens. Odd number. Until he saw the fourth, lying dead out on the rain-soaked grass. Long dead. Little more than a leather-skinned skeleton. Had it crawled out of the nest, lost its way and died alone? Or had the cat removed it when it died?

He stroked the cat sadly. She purred with pleasure, and didn't mind when he picked up a kitten; though she mewed and watched him anxiously. The kitten felt light as a bird in his hand. White and ginger, like its mother. Its dark eyes watched him, lively enough. He returned it, and the cat licked it back toward her nipples.

The second kitten seemed much the same; thin, but O.K.

The third did not have its eyes open. They were stuck up with terrible green stuff that spilled down its cheeks, almost to its mouth. Unlike the others, it squealed with pain and terror, and writhed in his hand. He thought of the first-aid kit, back in Mum's duffle bag, back in the mill. . . . But he knew cure was beyond him. Even if he could mix clean water and TCP, he could never stand the squealing while he bathed those eyes. . . .

Mum.

But it wasn't just Mum. It was bloody Jane and bloody

72

Joe Moreton too. Did Moreton have to follow Mum wherever she went, like a bloody puppy dog? Did he have to stand there, hovering like a helpless flabby ape, opening and closing his hands in misery, while Mum looked sorrowfully at the blind kitten?

"It'll have to be put down," said Mum, finally. Sad, but businesslike. "We can probably save the other two, but this one's too far gone. If we'd only found them a week ago. . . ."

"No, no, NO!" Simon stormed at her, in a rage of tears, knowing Joe Moreton was watching with those great gloomy eyes and hating him for it. "There's injections. . . ."

"Even vets can't work miracles," said Mum. "It'll always be blind. You wouldn't want it to live on, blind."

A great agony burst out of Simon; a great hatred of death that left him shaking, like an empty torn envelope. "Why *shouldn't* it live blind? We can look after it. It doesn't have to go out of the house. It's got the right to live, even blind. . . . If it doesn't want to live, it can always choose to die. But it can eat and drink and we can stroke it. . . . If we hadn't found it, it would have gone on living . . . we came here and interfered and *killed* it. *We're* the murderers. . . ."

"You really want it to live, even if it's blind?" asked Joe Moreton.

"Yes, yes, YES!" It was the first time Simon had ever looked Joe Moreton straight in the face.

"O.K.," said Joe Moreton. "But you look after it. We might find homes for the others, but that's *your* cat."

"You pair of soft buggers," said Mum. "I just hope it won't get dumped like your poor hamsters."

73

Simon carried the mother cat. Mum carried the kittens in her garden trug. The cat didn't seem to mind, provided Simon carried her where she could see the kittens. She only mewed anxiously when the kittens squeaked. Joe Moreton walked behind carrying Jane, who was, as usual when she was being carried, sucking her thumb; but asking why an animal doctor was called a vet, then announcng she was going to be the greatest vet in the world, and cure nel-lephants in the jungle.

There was a nasty moment at the real vet's. He made no fuss about the mother and the healthy kittens, though he shot them so full of injections, he made the kittens squeal. But he made all kinds of professional fuss about the blind kitten; hinted at dooms too awful to mention. But the whole family just stood and glared, and Joe Moreton said, with a return of his old sharpness, that *he* was paying. . . . The vet obviously thought them all mad; but they drove home together in the Range Rover, glad of their own madness. Simon was sent to get a new cardboard box from Cosima's, the village shop. And Mum turned the kitchen into something that felt very like a hospital.

Simon didn't mention starting up the mill; happily, nobody had noticed a thing.

9

SIMON SPENT THE AFTERNOON being glad. Roamed the garden, poked the soil, climbed several apple trees and occasionally looked over the gate down the road. But his mind wasn't really on it; he was too busy being glad. He kept nipping into the kitchen. But the cat and kittens were always asleep, in their new box by the Aga. The cat wouldn't even wake up when he opened a can of ham and held it under her nose; though her nose twitched. Finally Mum threw him out. But he didn't stop being glad.

It was about four when he heard the creaking in the road; and a singing. Not a kind of singing he'd ever heard before. Deep, huge and sonorous, like a cathedral organ on the march.

> *Rock of Ages, cleft for me,*
> *Let me hide myself in Thee.*

Any cleft would have needed to be as big as Grand Canyon, Arizona, for the creaking was from a wheelbarrow, and the barrow was being pushed by a huge old man. He rammed the gate open, removing a long sliver of white paintwork without worrying in the least.

He was a sandwich of an old man. His middle very ancient; an old man's jacket hung unbuttoned in rigid folds under his armpits, dragged down by pocketfuls of string, trowels and wooden pegs. But his legs were clad in faded jeans, and his feet in filthy training shoes. From the hips down he looked like a long-shanked teenager. And above the jacket, his white hair was cut short, almost skinhead. Brown skinhead face too; long, leathery and hard, with deep grooves round mouth and forehead.

He progressed along the crazy-paving path toward Simon. The wheel of his barrow gave a little wiggle to avoid Simon's outstretched feet. But no other acknowledgment was given. He proceeded to the nearest flower bed, sat in his wheelbarrow (making the wheel sink a good four inches into the earth) and slowly rolled a cigarette with an orange plastic device. Since the device was very small, and the man's fingers large, the end product was thin, measly and bent in the middle. Still, he stuck it in his mouth and patted his bulging pockets for matches.

No rattle rewarded him. He patted again, looking at Simon. Simon stared back, silently.

"Gorra match, son?"

"No," said Simon.

The man looked at the house hopefully. Simon looked with him, but there was no one in sight. The man puffed and tutted.

Simon ignored the hint; went on staring at him inscrutably. The man looked toward the gate, as if considering whether to go home for a match. Then he looked at his fag, wondering whether to throw it away. The wheelbarrow settled another inch, under his indignant bottom-wiggling.

"You his or hers?" asked the man.

"Hers," said Simon.

"Proper gentry, *she* is. Always a word. Don't get many o' her sort, round here."

"I'll get you a match," said Simon.

The man lit his wretched fag, and started to put the matchbox in his pocket. Simon held out his hand. The man took out a few matches and handed back the box, a new glint of respect in his eye.

"Home from school then? Wheer's tha dad?"

"Dead. He was a major. Killed in Aden."

"Ah. 'Tis always the good officers go fust."

"Were you a soldier?"

76

"Aye, in Fust War. Jerry sniper saved me life."

"Saved your life?"

"Aye—nineteen-futten. In a brickyard near Arras. Jerries were at one end, us on t'other. Not enough room to fight nor die. Tom Mercyfull, I said to meself, you'll not last t'day. Not enough time to mek your will. Any road, us had no dinner till four o'clock, then just tea and bully beef, one tin to every three lads. Us were passin' t'mugs round, between t'piles o' bricks, when mine jumped a yard in t'air. I looked an' saw it lying theer, wi' a hole right through it and tea spillin' out, and a finger still stuck through t'handle. Theer's a finger, I said. What's a finger doing theer wi' no hand? An' corporal said, it's thy finger, Tom. An' I was spoutin' blood all down me tunic an' feeling nowt. The major said, it's Blighty for you, Tom Mercyfull, an' thank your stars t'corporal saw it happen, otherwise ye coulda been on a court-martial on a charge o' self-wounding . . . right nasty he was, an' looking to be nastier."

"Self-wounding?"

"Aye, lots o' lads tried that in Fust War. Shootin' theirselves in fut or hand, to get out on a battle. But corporal had seen what happened and there was no getting past that. An' a rifleman isn't no good wi'out his trigger finger." He waggled his right hand, showing a rounded shiny-red stump. "They put me on hosses after that, which were a lot healthier nor brickyards. But they soon got rid on me altogether. I answered back too much for a sowger."

His fag had gone out. He pulled it out of his mouth, broke it in disgust and threw it among the rose trees. Then heaved himself out of his wheelbarrow. "Can't sit here talking all day." He began hoeing weeds; then tried to pick

77

them up with a rake, but they kept falling off. Simon wondered why he was doing it that way; then realized he couldn't bend at the hips.

"I'll do that," Simon offered.

"What's in it for you?"

"I'm a stranger round here. I like hearing you talk."

"Fair enough." Mr. Mercyfull stood with his head on one side, like a singer asked for an encore, considering his repertoire. Then he launched forth. "Most of me life I were a hoss brekker. Me father was a hoss brekker an' all."

"What's a hoss brekker?"

"Some hosses wun't wok—bone idle. Lovely hosses too, most on 'em. Ye could pick 'em out at hoss fairs 'cause their price was too low—owners trying to dump 'em—but word got round. Me dad would buy 'em up at rock-bottom price, and tek 'em home and put 'em in t' old hoss mill. Wheer a pair o' hosses had to walk round and round in a circle, wokkin' t'millstone for grindin' corn. We had another hoss that were a grand wokker. But the idle hoss, he would just stand theer, not movin', tryin' it on. . . . Me dad were a hard man—he'd use t'whip, throw buckets o' watter over it, hold a bit o' burning wood to its head— even put a Guy Fawkes cracker up its arse—anything to get it moving. I've seen 'im have our other hoss drag it round by main force, hooves trailin'.

"Them hosses allus wokked in t'end—they was glad to. Then we could sell 'em for a grand price. Mercyfull's hosses was guaranteed to wok or bring 'em back. It were a kindness really—though I don't suppose yer RSPCA would think so today. But if we hadna brokken 'em, they'd a gone for cats' meat, an' what sort o' kindness is that?"

Mr. Mercyfull bridged sixty years with a sigh. Then said, shrewdly, "What do ye think of yon feller then?" He nodded at the house.

"Oh. . . ." Simon couldn't help his feelings showing, though he knew it was bad form in front of a man like Mercyfull.

"I *thowt* so," said Mr. Mercyfull. "A right rum 'un. Meks out he were born in this place, an' he weren't. He come from Manchester in t' Second War, a bairn in his ma's arms. And he were gone off to grammar school afore he were twelve. An' we didna see him again till he brings yer mam, an' starts spendin' money like watter an' playin' Mr. Big. Drawing pictures in books—what kind o' job is that for a grown man?"

Simon grunted doubtfully, a bit guilty since Joe had been so decent about the cat.

"Thowt so," said Mr. Mercyfull again, triumphantly. "Ye can't stand 'im either, can ye? Marryin' a lady like yer mam. Anybody can see he's not gentry, just be lookin' at 'im. Got a lot o' money an' don't know the value on't. When he was havin' this place done up—I can tell ye one or two ways them builders stung 'im. An' him too busy to notice, followin' yer mam round like a slavering lapdog."

Simon nearly said, "He can't help what he is." But he didn't want Mr. Mercyfull thinking him soft. So he just said, "I must go and do something," and walked off into the kitchen.

Jane was busy coloring in a map of Middle-earth, with about three hundred felt-tips.

"Where's Mum?" asked Simon.

"Probably having a little lie-down," said Jane, not looking up. "She usually does. Gets tired with all the extra housework—it's a very big house."

"Oh." He felt unaccountably desolate.

" 'Spect Joe's gone for a lie-down too. They won't be long." Her tongue slid round the corner of her mouth, as her felt-tip slid round a corner of her picture.

Desperation seized Simon. He stared at the door that led to the stairs that led to Mum's bedroom.

" 'Sno good," said Jane. "They always lock the door. They won't be long." She gave him a sly peep from under her lashes. "Why don't you like Joe, Simon? He's *nice*."

"What do you mean, *nice?*"

"Big an' cuddly an' all hairy—he tickles you an' makes you laugh. He gives us wet sloppy kisses and Mum and me say *pooh*."

The devils sang in the air. His palms turned sweaty; his hair prickled. He saw again the bathroom door at school— the smashed door with the shocking star of splintered wood, and inside, Bowdon making disgusting noises.

"I don't just not like Joe Moreton—I *hate* him!"

"Why, Simon, why?" Her juicy slyness was gone. Eyes as big as saucers. Face starting to pucker up.

"Because-he-is-not-my-father."

"Well, he is *my* father an' I love him—you hear? I *love* him!" Her voice rose to a shriek.

"You never knew Father—he died before you were born. But he *was* your father. Little traitor. . . ." He was yelling too, at the top of his voice.

Jane threw a felt-tip. A red felt-tip. It made a red mark on his white shirt. She threw another, and another. . . .

80

He let go; let the devils in. Ran. Not to the bedroom door; to the mill.

The moment he left the house, Mum burst into the kitchen, a woolen sock in one hand, and a darning needle in the other. "*Whatever* is going on?"

A door banged open upstairs and Joe Moreton appeared, thickly laden paintbrush in his hand. "What's up?"

"It's Simon. He's gone potty," said Jane huffily.

"What about?" asked Mum, picking up the scattered felt-tips.

"I don't know," said Jane. "He just *is* potty. I *hate* him."

"But what *happened?*"

"I threw my felt-tips at him."

"If we try to get to the bottom of every quarrel . . ." said Joe, with a bored sigh. He picked her up. She immediately slipped her thumb into her mouth.

"Don't do that, Jane," said Mum.

"Want to!"

Out in the garden, Mr. Mercyfull watched Simon go, thoughtfully. Then he settled into his wheelbarrow and took out his little orange device.

Simon knew nothing until he was sitting at the wooden table, on the wooden chair, twisting the rough-bitten wooden pipe from the tabletop between his hands, round and round. Smelling the acid smell of bare earth coming up through the floorboards from the cellar. His hands and legs were stinging all over; from rose trees and nettles he must have crashed into without even noticing.

The mill was silent, cool, green. The silence and the coolness and the greenness dripped into his empty aching mind, slowly filling it with peace. He was grateful to the mill; he did not resist. There was nothing else to fill his mind with, that was not agony.

He looked round at everything slowly and in great detail, as his breathing grew quieter and the shuddering in his body stopped. How he loved everything here . . . if only the cat and kittens had still been here. But Mum and Joe Moreton and that rotten little cow Jane had taken even the cat and kittens away from him. Still, he had the coats hanging there on the wall; and the hats above them. If only their owners were still here. *They* would be kind. . . . He went on staring hungrily at the coats, till he laid his head on his hands and fell asleep.

He came awake with a start. He had no idea what time it was, but the room was a lot darker; it must be late. He had a sense of being watched, of being watched over; coming from the left. He glanced round—and thought for a moment that three people were standing in the shadowed corner, watching. The same three people. It made him leap inside his skin.

But it was only the coats. Or a dream; or the coming out of a dream. Just coats hanging on a wall, and hats on pegs.

All the same, he left the mill quickly, without even pausing to shut the door properly behind him.

"Foxes," said Mr. Mercyfull. "Foxes is cunning devils, specially she-vixens. Yer dog-fox is a straight crook, but yer she-vixen. . . ."

Yesterday's hoeing had been abandoned, and he was now digging the rosebed with about as much enthusiasm. Simon watched as he let go his spade and proceeded to straighten his back. This was a long process, involving putting his hands in the small of it, and heaving upward. Rather like a cross between a housewife doing keep-fit and an old gray wolf baying at the moon. He creaked, then cracked, then sighed with relief and lowered himself into the barrow.

"I mind one January I were hedging our bottom field, 'cause it were too cold for owt else. An' I see this she-vixen come running by, lookin' ower her showlder. And she goes an' sits in t'middle o' a frozen pond, bold as brass. An' I thowt, what's up here, then? I soon knowed, 'cause I heard t' Hunt coming. But she still held her ground, bold as brass, till hounds came swarming all ower me and onto t'ice. Then she skipped onto t'far bank, and they nearly had her when t'ice gave way wi' a greet crack, and the whole pack went down into it. Aye, ye could see t'hounds down under t'ice, blowing greet bubbles.

"An' then huntsmen arrived, and they fetched ladders an' laid 'em across t' ice. An' Lord Herdsmere, who were Lord Knutsford's son, crawled out on the ladders hisself in his scarlet coat to try an' save them, but it weren't no good. They all drowned but four, who came ashore theirselves, being on t'edge when ice went. An' the old vixen sat on a wall, just watching it all an' laughing wi' her tongue out. Till Lord Herdsmere sent a man for a gun, then she slipped away sharp. Lord Herdsmere were a hard man an' proud—gie ye a whip across yer face as soon as look at ye—but he were blabbin' like a bairn that day. Tears running down his face an' freezin', an' they say he never hunted again.

"But I ask you—how did yon she-vixen know t' ice were that thin? *I* didn't know, and I were hedgin' there."

He began to roll one of his awful cigarettes.

"Aye, but she were too fond o' that pond in the end. I seed her sitting on its bank soon after, an' there was two dog-foxes fightin' over her, on t'ice, and her sitting there watchin' an' enjoyin' every minute. I had me gun with me, an' I lined them up an' got all three wi' one shot. An' they were so intent on what they was doing that they never even knew I was theer." Mr. Mercyfull gave a deep sigh, at the satisfying state of the world.

"Did you do it," asked Simon, "to revenge the hounds?"

"No. I cared nowt for hounds nor hunt. Them foxes had taken too many of my chickens."

"Why *do* they call you Mercyfull?" asked Simon.

"It's a twisting o' the name. They say our real name were Merseyfield—a field by the River Mersey, up a bit north. Some says we were really Vikings."

"Yes," said Simon. Then added, almost against his will, "What kind of name is Moreton?"

"Oh, Moreton's a local name enough—there's a Little Moreton Hall just down t'road—a greet black-and-white place wick wi' tourists. But yon feller come from Manchester wi' his ma in 1940—evacuees, *she* said. There never were no da showed up—his ma made out she were a widow; but nobody ever dared ask to see her marriage license. . . ."

Mr. Mercyfull spat accurately at a butterfly hovering between the rose bushes; but the butterfly dodged craftily, like they always do.

Simon lay in his attic bedroom in the dark. They had packed him right away at the top of the house. There had been no need to. The place had plenty of rooms in its long funny shape. Downstairs, the lounge, facing the road, with its huge new picture window in the gable end. Then the entrance hall, then the dining room, with the kitchen beyond that, then the scullery, then the door through to the newly built two-car garage at the back.

Upstairs on the first floor, a long corridor with four bedrooms off it, and Joe Moreton's huge new studio at the back, over the huge new garage. A funny house, five rooms long and one room wide, if you didn't count the corridor . . . and him alone up on the top floor in the attic, up a tiny narrow stair with doors at the top and bottom of it.

He'd taken to coming to bed early. He couldn't stand the cosy huddle round the telly. But then he felt so lonely he got into the habit of leaving both the staircase doors open and playing his records very loudly. Mum came up sometimes to tell him to shut the doors and turn the record player down; but she never stayed to talk. Then he would go down to the bathroom, and on the way back he would leave all the doors open all over again. . . .

But now all was silent. He'd heard Mum look in on Jane at eleven, then cross the hall to her own bedroom, below his. He'd strained his ears for noises, but heard nothing. The old house was built very thick.

All around him in the dark lay his old toys. His big models of a Super-fortress and a Lancaster, a Stirling and a Liberator had even been hung tastefully from the ceiling beams when he first arrived. Just as he liked them.

He had carefully moved them all to different positions. He had a shrewd idea who had arranged them. Mum hadn't a clue about flying; she'd have hung them all crashing into each other. What else had Joe Moreton fingered, looked at sarcastically, messed about with his big banana fingers? It made everything perfectly useless; even if not a thing had been thrown away or broken . . . he had checked double carefully.

Even in this old attic, there was the smell of Joe Moreton; the smell of woodworm-killer from the beams, the smell of new paint and expensive Vymura, the smell of Joe Moreton's money. Simon felt so lonely it was like freezing to death slowly.

Only one thing that Joe Moreton wouldn't have dared touch: Father's kit. It lay in a white cupboard in the corner—a cupboard built in as part of the house. A cupboard that had been there a hundred years before Joe Moreton. He crept out of bed; he would lay his head against the two bulging holdalls that held Father's kit; holdalls with Father's name, rank, number and regiment stenciled on the outside.

105692 MAJ D. E. WOOD, ROYAL DURHAM FUSILIERS. Derek Edward Wood, M.C.

The canvas would be a harsh comfort to his cheek. It only smelled of canvas now, no longer of Father; but it was better than smelling of Joe Moreton. He opened the cupboard door, and gasped.

There was a tiny oval of light inside the cupboard, shining on one of the holdalls, illuminating the MAJ.

He glanced over his shoulder, expecting a trick; expecting Jane had crept up on him and was shining a pencil torch over his shoulder. But there was no one there. The room was completely dark, except for the faint blue squares of the window. In a panic, he slammed the cupboard shut and fled back to bed.

But the cupboard door, not properly latched, swung slowly open. He could still see the oval of light, quite clear.

He wondered if it would leave the cupboard and somehow start moving around the room. He wondered if the oval light had something to do with Father; Father come back to look after him? If it *was* Father's ghost, he wouldn't mind at all. He would welcome it, really he would. . . .

But long though he watched the little oval of light, half-hopeful, half-petrified, it did not move. He would have to go to *it*.

He crept toward it on legs that shook disgustingly. Squatted and stared, closer and closer. It still did not move. Just showed up the rough weave of the canvas.

He reached out and touched it. His finger threw a shadow on it, upward. It was ordinary light. From where?

The floor of the cupboard. On the dark plank floor shone a tiny gold jewel of brilliance. Nothing more than a hole in the old planks, and the light of the bedroom below, shining up through. He pushed the kitbags aside, and put his eye to the hole. All he could see was flowered wallpaper, a white skirting board and a piece of blue carpet.

With a bra of Mum's thrown down on it. Not like her, that. She was normally so tidy with her clothes. All neatly folded on a chair, when he had gone to her room in the night; when he'd felt sick or had toothache or something.

She *used* to be tidy. . . .

Then he heard her voice. "Happy?" Her voice, all gooey and dreamy, like treacle.

Rumble. Big fat rumble from big fat hairy chest.

Simon leaped away as if he'd been stung. He wasn't an eavesdropper. He hadn't meant to listen. Just been curious about the light. Besides, listening hurt so much; he would never, never, never listen again.

Within two minutes he was back to the hole. He could put his ear right against it, though it made his neck ache and the sill of the bottom of the cupboard bit into his collar bone.

"It was worse tonight." Joe Moreton's voice. "There we were, all three of us snug round the telly, and all I could think about was him upstairs. Like a bloody death in the house."

"Yes," said Mum.

"D'you think he's doing it deliberately? I don't want to seem paranoid—"

"Oh yes, he's doing it deliberately. Trying to upset you. He never used to be like that; he used to bring his records downstairs and play them. Nearly drove me mad with the noise, but he wanted to share them, then. Bloody awful things. Led Zeppelin. But he sees something in them. He used to try to make me see it."

Joe Moreton sighed, and the bed creaked as he turned over. "By God, I used to think it rough when I was broke. When I first left art school and was washing up in Lyon's

Cornerhouses all night and tramping round Fleet Street all day, and drawing when I could hardly stay awake. But that all seems so simple now. . . . Then when I hit what I shall mockingly call the Big Time, and the money was pouring in, I thought, well . . . I thought, things can never be so bad again. But *this!*"

"I told you we shouldn't get married. You could have laid low in his holidays—the rest would have been O.K."

"No, Deb, you know I didn't want that. Besides, you get tired of driving home in the middle of the night. I need something to cuddle permanently on tap. And your shiny face at breakfast. And Jane. . . ."

"Oh, I knew you'd have no bother with Jane. She's man-mad. You never think they can be sexy at that age. Always hanging round my chair when I was getting ready to go out, wanting a bit of perfume, bit of lipstick. She wanted me to have you for what she could get out of it. She never stops trying to steal you off me, sexy little beast. But that's no problem."

Joe Moreton sighed. "It's a laugh really. All this talk of domineering parents, ruining their kids' lives. Nobody says you're the prisoners of your children."

"There speaks the old bachelor. Where have you been, these last twenty years?"

"Making me way, missus. . . ."

"Was there never any other woman . . . ?"

"I've *told* you. When you're going places, you travel light. Mainly on account of your empty belly—"

"You haven't got an empty belly *now*."

"Ow. Lay off, sadist! Blame your own cooking. I used to have a figure like a long-distance runner. . . ."

"I'm not grumbling. You suit me as you are."

"Stop it, will you? Lay off!"

Giggly laughter floated up through the hole in the floorboards. Then silence. Then Mum said, "Mmmmmmmm," appreciatively.

"Shall I bugger off? Till the end of his holidays?"

Simon's heart leaped for joy.

"No," said Mum, and she really meant it. "That's exactly what he wants. And it would be very bad for him if he got it. Letting him drive you out of your own house? He'd be intolerable for the rest of his life."

"I'm not scared of him. I'm scared *for* him. He's so bloody lonely—it fills the whole house, like the smell of a leaky toilet."

"It's not just you—he's always been lonely. Even when he was little, he'd never really let you get through to him. Like his father; like Derek. *He'd* never stop still and let you touch him either."

"We're all a bit locked up inside, I suppose."

"*You?* Locked up inside? That's really funny. You're the one that lets it all hang out—you're the easiest person to touch I know. Why do you think I fell for you—your classic good looks?" She was laughing again. A contented gurgling that went though Simon like a spear. "You're the best thing that ever happened to me, Joe."

"Even with . . . all this?"

"Even with all this. I'm *worried*—but to be without you now would be unthinkable. Kiss me, you silly sod."

Another long silence, with nothing of despair or loneliness in it. Then Mum said, "Again? Joe—not *again!*" Then the terrible undecipherable animal noises, surging to peaks and falling, like the waves of the sea. Then Mum crying,

"Joe. Joe. Joe. Joe!" as if she were gladly falling off a cliff into some warm bottomless dark.

For nearly an hour, Simon remained crouched by the cupboard, head between his knees and hands over his ears. Every so often he would rock backward and forward gently. Then be motionless again.

After an hour he listened for the snores below, then got up calmly and carefully closed the cupboard door, crept into bed and stared at the ceiling until morning.

11

"I'VE BEEN THINKING," said Joe Moreton, "about the kid." Simon was once again crouched over the cupboard. He had given up feeling guilty about eavesdropping; no longer cared. "I got through to him once, you know. I swear. Over that kitten. He really looked at me like I was human. 'Cause *I* was taking him seriously. Maybe he thinks I don't like him. I mean, nowadays I can hardly bring myself to speak to him, or even look at him. Maybe he's getting the wrong message."

"Don't be thick, Joe. He knows exactly what's on your mind. You're as open as a book."

"Oh, I don't know . . . I'm not always like I am with you. I can be very sarcastic. . . ."

"Only with strangers. You're like a lobster—all armor outside and soft as hell inside. I should know."

"But does he?"

"Don't think everyone's like you. He's not. He's hard *inside*."

91

"Nobody's that hard inside. I keep feeling so sorry for him. I'd like to give him a present."

"What *sort* of present?" Mum's voice, suddenly sharp, worried.

"Saw a smashing bike in Knutsford—racer, alloy frame, six gears—schoolboy's dream. What kid could resist?"

"This kid. Oh, Joe, the whole point about that terrible old boneshaker he rides is that his father used to ride it. He'll keep it, down to the last speck of rust."

"O.K. Let him. Doesn't mean he can't have a new one as well . . . he could ride both. No harm trying, is there?"

"Joe, Joe, you can't buy love."

"Anybody'd given me a bike when I was a kid, I'd have loved them forever. Even if it was a mass of rust. Trouble with that kid is, he's never known what it's like to go without."

Mum's voice grew sharper. "Leave it, Joe. He'd only use it to screw you. Refuse to ride it, leave it out in the rain, smash it to pieces."

Joe Moreton suddenly flared. "I don't know. We've tried playing it your way. Where's it got us? Things just get worse and worse. What's going to be the end of it? C'mon, what do you see as the end of it? What you got in mind?"

Mum's voice went cold and dead. "I know what the end will be. He'll go to Wellington at the end of the holidays, and then we shall get some peace. Just the three of us again."

"What about Christmas? And when he leaves school?"

"He'll go away again. Into the Army. Globe trotting, just like his father. He'll come and see me twice a year. Christmas and my birthday; because it's his duty."

"God—how can you be so *heartless?* He's your kid."

And upstairs, Simon rocked backward and forward. Mum, Mum, it's not true. Mum, can't you see I want *you?* I need *you?*

"I'm not heartless, Joe. Just realistic. He's so like his father. . . . Derek was leaving me before he was killed. He'd really left already, I suppose. I've always wondered why it hurt so little, Derek's dying. Till now."

"Other women?"

"Nothing so human. I could have forgiven him that. No: horses and fast cars and parachutes and fighting. Any place he could risk his neck. It got to be a disease. My God, Derek certainly wasn't afraid of death; but I used to wonder whether he wasn't afraid of life."

"Afraid of *life?*"

"Afraid of going gray, getting old, coming home every night and letting the kids jump all over him while he was watching the telly. I suppose, even from the beginning, he was never really *with* me. Not like you, Joe. Every day. In bed."

"Was he queer or something?"

"No—he just *took* me, like I was another fence, another parachute jump. Then turned his back afterward and lay and smoked in the dark. I could never touch him, like—"

"Ouch! Leggo! I'll go on a diet next week. Promise."

"Look. I never knew what love was, till I met you. Fancy . . . married, two kids, thirty-three years old and *now* I have to find out. If I hadn't met you . . . poor Derek. You'd understand if you met Derek's father. Terrible old man. Derek used to take me to see him twice a year—as a duty. Christmas and his birthday. We just sat

93

around drinking Scotch and talking about the bloody regiment, because there was nothing else to do. And Derek as black as hell for a week afterward—riding like he *wanted* to break his neck."

"Why the hell'd you marry him?"

"My parents were pleased . . . I was nineteen and scared of being left on the shelf."

"How the other half lives. . . ."

"But–now–I–have–you–lovely–bastard." Her voice had gone treacly again.

Why did they have to keep *on* doing it? thought Simon.

Then: traitor, traitor, traitor!

Whore, whore, whore!

The words boomed through his mind like great gongs. Until his whole skull was a belfry for the words. The devils whispered. . . . He didn't even struggle. Threw open the door of his mind and welcomed them.

When he came back to himself, the kitbags from the cupboard were open and sagging in the pale dawn light. And all round the room, neatly arranged, were items of his father's kit. Dress blues on a chair, tunic draped across the back, peaked cap on the carefully folded trousers. Khaki on the bed, with the webbing belt, holster and revolver. A camouflaged para-jacket hung on the door and even shaving things on the wash basin.

He knew exactly what he had to do.

"Now you sure you'll be all right?" asked Mum. "We won't be late. I've left the phone number of The Bells of Peover on the pad. Any bother, and we can be back in five minutes."

Simon smiled up at her. "We'll be O.K. There's a good film on the telly. Have a nice time."

"See that Jane goes to bed by nine. Don't take any nonsense. Any later and you know how ratty she gets."

"Don't worry. I can handle Jane."

Mum kissed Jane good-night, with big ape Moreton queuing up for his kiss too. He, of course, got three, and a big hug, and jam on his face from the cream cake that Jane had conned out of Mum as blood money because she was going out for the evening.

"And see she cleans her teeth, Simon," said Mum.

"Yeah," said Simon, going back to his motor-racing magazine. Would they never push off? He had so much to do.

He listened to the Range Rover pull out of the drive.

"Play with me, Simon," said Jane.

He played with her; building enormous castles that somehow she always managed to knock down with a swish of her hair or the back of her hand, just as they were nearly finished. How mad that rotten little game used to make him. But he didn't care at all now.

"Are you feeling better now, Simon?" asked Jane. "Do you love Mum again?"

"Course I do." He concentrated very hard on putting the top on the castle.

"And do you love Joe now, as well?" Her voice was prying, wheedling. She was lying full length on the carpet, trying to peer up into his face because it was hidden by the curtain of his hair.

"He's all right, I suppose."

"Oh, no, he's *lovely*. Tell me he's lovely, Simon!"

95

"I said he was *all right*," Simon said, between clenched teeth.

"Tell you a secret about Joe?" wheedled Jane.

"*What?*" He looked up suddenly, and she flinched.

"I was only going to say . . . he's going to buy you a *big* bike."

"Really." Simon ducked his head again. Jane was a bloody sight too sharp. A lot harder to fool than grownups.

"Simon? You look different. You look *funny*."

"If I look funny," said Simon, "it's because you gave me a funny look."

"Si-mon. Be serious. Si-mon, what's the matter really? You can tell me. I can keep a secret."

Like hell, he thought. Little Miss Tittle-tattle. But he said, "You see this castle—it's the biggest and best I've ever built. 'Cause it's the Castle of Count Frankenstein, in Transylvania. . . ."

"Oh, *that*," she said. "I saw that on the telly. On Joe's knee. Mummy was ever so cross, but I didn't care. And Joe was much more frightened than me. But I hugged him tight and that made him feel better."

"But Frankenstein's not just on the telly. He was a real man; and he made a real monster out of bits and pieces. And then it got away and went potty, and Frankenstein had to destroy it and it destroyed him, and they all died. . . ."

Her hand came down so hard, the castle flew in a hundred pieces all over the carpet. He looked up, amazed at the violence. Her eyes were blazing, like Mum's. He'd never realized before how like Mum she was.

"I hate you!" said Jane. "You're *wicked*. You'll be sorry.

I'm not playing any more. Now put on the telly." And she went and composed herself in the big leather armchair. Joe Moreton's armchair. Its arms surrounded her; she made it actually look as if she was sitting on his knee. "And I want you to ring up Mummy, to come home. I don't want to be with *you* any more. And I shall tell her the *wicked* things you said."

He broke out in a sweat. The last thing he needed was them home now.

"Sorry, Jane," he said, in a voice so sugary it sickened him. "I was only fooling. Sorry I frightened you."

She gave him the same hard unforgiving stare. "You won't get round *me*. I know what you're doing. You go and ring up Mummy this minute, or I'll ring her up myself. I know where the number is. Even if you hide it, I can ask the op—erator."

She would too, little bitch. Or have hysterics if he tried to stop her; claw and bite and scratch until she was totally out of control. And tell Mum every detail when she got home. And *he* would be in the wrong. And how much did she know of what he was going to do? He'd packed all Father's kit away again, but she still might have seen it. She was always going to the bathroom in the middle of the night, and in the old days had often come into his room afterward, prising open his sleeping eyelids to wake him up. . . .

"Please, Jane, please. I really am sorry, I really am. Shall I get you an ice cream?"

She considered a long time. Ice cream was her weak spot. She could never get enough, and she was still just too small to lift the lid of the freezer herself. Her eyes ceased to be angry; now they were hard and wary. "A chocolate one . . . two chocolate ones . . . *three* chocolate ones. With six wafers."

"You'll make yourself sick!"

"Do as you're told, Simon!"

Did she really know anything? Had she been spying, following him? Or could she merely home in on his unease? You could never tell with Jane. Best to take no chances. He went to fetch it.

"And don't forget, I'm watching you," she said. "Always."

She was asleep at last. Teeth uncleaned, chocolate ice cream all over her face, and cherubically innocent-looking. There would be hell to pay in the morning, when Mum found her like that. But he couldn't wipe her face without waking her up again.

And then he smiled, a little sadly, at how childish he was being. Mum being mad about ice cream belonged in the far, far away past of Croydon. There would be a lot more hell to pay than an ice-creamy face. And it would be a long time before morning.

He gathered up the cleaning rags and the *Brasso*, and crept to his room. The smell of *Brasso* reminded him of Corporal Briggs, with his cropped hair, and the fag that stuck to his bottom lip, and the tales about Old Rommel. The smell of *Brasso* was safe and home. He shook the bottle like Corporal Briggs used to. Always shake the *Brasso* thoroughly, lad! Once, Corporal Briggs had sat too long drinking tea in Mum's kitchen, telling Mum for the hundredth time about Old Rommel, and then he had caught sight of the clock and knew it was too late to get ready Father's dress blues for the Mess that night. And Mum said Corporal Briggs would cop it and be on a fizzer. But Corporal Briggs had bet Mum a bob he wouldn't; he knew a thing or two. . . .

And Corporal Briggs had just laid out Father's kit uncleaned; but taken the loose change from Father's pockets and polished up the pennies till they shone like silver and laid them out in a pattern on top of Father's trousers. And Father had been so pleased with the shining pennies, he'd never noticed the kit was dirty, and went on and on about what a thorough chap Corporal Briggs was. And Mum had laughed afterward, and paid Corporal Briggs his bob. But it was all right for Corporal Briggs to fool Father, because Corporal Briggs loved Father and would have died for him. He often said so. Not like *some* people. . . . Simon's face hardened. Two deep narrow lines appeared on his forehead that Father would have recognized. Very thoroughly, he began to clean the blackened metal on Father's dress blues.

When he was finished and satisfied, he carried the clothes and the highly polished boots down to Mum's bedroom, and arranged them neatly on and under the bedside chair. It was funny how you didn't forget things, even after eight years. . . .

He sat on his bed in the dark. When he heard the Range Rover, he looked at the luminous hands of his watch. Half past ten. At least she had kept her word about not being late. He moved across to the hole in the cupboard. There was no patch of light; the room below was in darkness.

He heard them in the hall downstairs.

99

"He's gone to bed," said Joe Moreton.

"I can't say I'm sorry," said Mum. "For once I feel great. I wouldn't want to spoil it."

"He seemed better . . . this evening."

"Optimist!"

"I'm always optimistic when I'm a bit tight," said Joe Moreton. "Optimistic and amorous. Hadn't you noticed?"

"Why d'you think *I* drove us home?" But she didn't seem cross; that giggly note was back in her voice.

"Me for *bed*," said Joe, pleased at her giggle.

"I won't be a minute, love," said Mum. "I'll just look at Jane."

"Don't be lo-ong."

"I wo-on't."

He heard Mum's quick foot on the stairs, and got into bed, just in case. But Mum just closed Jane's door, and went along the corridor. So he nipped quickly out to the cupboard again.

"I haven't put the overhead light on," said Joe Moreton, sighing luxuriously. "Only the bedside. More romantic."

"You're *incorrigible*."

"Thank you for the new gear," said Joe.

"What new gear?" asked Mum.

"The policeman's set in the chair. I'm not sure it'll fit me, though."

"What policeman's set?" For a moment, Mum sounded puzzled.

Then silence. Silence that went on and on, worse than a great terrible scream. Silence that seemed to echo and echo round the old house.

Silence and silence and silence.

Finally, Joe Moreton's voice, wobbling all over the

place. "What's the matter, love? For God's sake, what's the matter? What's the *matter?* WHAT'S THE MATTER? Speak to me. You look like—Deb, what is the matter?"

Still silence. And Joe Moreton flapping round like a wet hen, still trying to get her to tell him what the matter was.

Upstairs, Simon crouched, smiling, feeling like a god. We did it, Father. We did it.

Until the door was flung open and the light crashed on, and a pair of huge hands grabbed him with unheeding savagery and carried him bodily downstairs, banging his head again and again in the process. So strong and brutal were the hands that Simon was quite sure he was going to die. . . . Well, he'd die happy, after that.

But the hands merely dumped him down in front of Mum, though they kept their vicious grip. Mum was crouched on the bed, shrunken, looking lined and cold as an old woman. Simon could not read the expression in her eyes. They were lost eyes.

"Tell her what you did," said Joe Moreton in an awful voice. "Tell her what you did, you despicable little sod." And he shook Simon like a rat.

But Simon made himself stand up straight. Shook the great ape-hands off. He looked at his mother.

"I cleaned Father's kit and put it there. To remind you he still exists, you whore." He had thought carefully what to say while waiting in the dark.

Something hit him, and he ended on his knees in the corner of the room.

"Whore," he shouted. "Whore, whore, *whore!*"

Joe Moreton came at him again. He prepared to die with dignity.

"Stop!" said Mum. She got to her feet, and came across

101

to Simon. "Bring those clothes, Joe. Come upstairs, Simon."

Up in the attic, she opened the kitbag and stuffed the clothes back in, as if they were jumble. She never noticed the hole in the floor of the cupboard. Then she said, "Take those things downstairs, please. Joe. And lock them in your studio."

Simon went mad then, clawing for the kitbags. "They're mine, mine, mine! My father left them to me. By law."

"When you are twenty-one," said Mum. "When you are grown-up enough to use them *properly* and with *respect*."

Simon clung to the canvas desperately, but Joe Moreton pulled his hands away, and walked to the door, one bag under each great arm.

"I hate you!" screamed Simon. "I hate you both."

"And I think I hate you as well," said Joe Moreton, quietly. "I just hope one day I can get over it."

"Where are they going? Where are you taking them?"

"They're going to Nunk," said Mum. "They'll be quite safe with Nunk. Nunk will know what to do."

12

SIMON SAT WEAKLY ON THE edge of his bed. His rage had been flattened by the rage of Joe Moreton. His head ached where Moreton had banged it against doors and banisters; his shoulders ached where Moreton had gripped- them. His lip was cut, where Moreton had slapped him right across the room. And yet Joe Moreton had not really done it for hate; he had done it like a great hurricane, without hate. All Joe Moreton had done, he had done because Mum had been hurt. You had to be fair; you had to admit that.

Just for a moment, Simon felt he'd done wrong. He'd thought Joe Moreton a great slobby lump; and Joe had not been a great slobby lump. Joe Moreton at least was a man. . . . And he remembered that look on Mum's face: as if she was being murdered . . . and he *was* sorry, in a way.

But they had done wrong to Father. And now they had bundled Father away like he was jumble. Father had been far away enough; and now they were taking him away even further. Eight years, before he could even touch Father's things again. That was *wrong*.

He had done wrong; but they had done far greater wrong.

Slowly, reluctantly, as if drawn by some force stronger than himself, he went back to the hole in the cupboard. He had to know; he had to know what they were doing, saying.

"Drink it down," Joe Moreton was saying. "Get it down you—it'll make it hurt less."

"I can't stand whisky. It always makes me sick."

"Me too. But get it down."

Mum made gulping noises.

"What we going to do?" asked Joe Moreton. "What we going to do with him?"

"Don't talk about him like that; he is my son."

"I could kill him."

"No, you couldn't. You're not a killer, Joe. I should know. I married into a whole breed of killers. Quiet, cool, decently behaved killers. Killers who will tip their hat to a lady, go to church because it's church parade, are decent

103

with horses, cry over a dead dog, and kill because it's their duty. For King and Country. Derek had killed men, you know—that one in Aden . . . Cyprus, Borneo . . . Trucial Oman. He never talked about it. But I knew. You should have seen him handling a gun at the grouse shooting. So efficient . . . I could have screamed. And his father . . . that dreadful old man . . . you heard tales . . . a riot in India during Partition. He had to put it down . . . law and order . . . a few too many got killed and he—retired early. Never really got over it. Oh, the Woods are bred for it—like foxhounds—generation after generation. I used to think there was probably a Wood at the Battle of Hastings. And in peacetime, they get so bored . . . I don't blame them . . . society breeds them."

"And what do we do about *this* little killer upstairs?"

"*I* don't know. I'm tired now. Leave it till morning."

"I'm not going to let him kill *you*. I'll have him put away first."

"You couldn't. He's not mad. Anyway, we will put him away—to school."

"That's five weeks, yet. What do we do in the meanwhile? Build barricades? Put up barbed wire? He's not safe to have around. He could set fire to the house when we're all asleep."

"He'll not do that—that's *illegal*."

"There's plenty he could do that's not illegal. It's like living with a time bomb."

"There is . . ." said Mum hesitantly, doubtfully.

"Yes?"

"There is one person who might be able to deal with him . . . it's only a thin hope."

104

"Who?"

"Not now. Let me sleep on it. I think I could sleep now."
Mum yawned.

"I'll lock that bloody door."

"He won't try anything else tonight. . . ."

And, fools, they were soon snoring like pigs. Full of
whisky. But at least they hadn't made the noises. He'd
stopped that; for tonight. He wondered, wolfishly, whether
there was something else he could do, while they slept.
It seemed too good a chance to miss. But when he got to
his feet, he found his legs and arms shook so violently, he
could hardly move. And the terrible uncaring strength of
Joe Moreton's hands had taken away his courage. He was
good for nothing more.

Except to limp downstairs, and out through the back
door.

The night was dark; only a few stars breaking through
swirling clouds. The grass of the orchard was soaking, and
squelched and slipped under his bare feet. There was still
rain in the wind.

He went and stood at the gate that led to the turnip field.
Drops spattered on him from the sodden hedge, every time
the wind blew. He could smell, overpoweringly, the rich
smell of wet turnips; and something deeper and danker
beyond: the smell of the mill pool. Though he did not
realize what it was.

Then he did something he'd done sometimes before.
Waited for the constellation of the Plough and the Pole
Star to appear, through a gap in the dark blanks of cloud.
That gave him north. Father had shown him how to do
that; taking him out in his arms on a night when the whole

105

sky was full of stars like a great city of lamps. Father saying, "If you ever get lost in the dark, Simon, look for the Pole Star. That will see you home."

He marked a tree branch that lay directly under the Pole Star, so that when the Pole Star disappeared behind the clouds again, he still had north. Then he pointed his whole arm toward north, stiffly out leftward from his body.

Now he was facing east. But Father wasn't buried east; east was Moscow. Father was buried south-east; or east-by-south, actually. He'd worked it out carefully from an atlas. . . . He jiggled about, bare feet on wet grass, like a man aiming a gun. When he was finally settled, he was facing directly toward where Father was buried.

And then he closed his eyes, so the whole blackness round him swayed, and he heard the lonely sound of the wind rushing through the trees.

And then he recited the line of poetry that Slogger had taught them.

> *He rides the wild October sky; he shall not die, he shall not die.*

Even though it was only August, it worked any month.

And then he spoke to his father.

"They're too strong. They have taken you away. They are too big for me. Come. Help me. Come. Come. *Come.*"

He could feel the devils cluster round him, under the trees, singing in the air, and he went out of himself, still chanting: *"Help me, help me. Come."*

And it seemed to him that something answered. It did not feel like Father; but how could he know what Father was like, now? He shuddered, but remained steadfast. He gave the Something a permission to intervene. Then he stirred, sighed, feeling emptier than ever. Yawned like a child and went back into the house. He did not lock the back door. That would have seemed like changing his mind about the invitation; and it was too late to change his mind.

Far away, the desert dawn wind blew through a British Military Cemetery. Neglected; unlike most. Surrounded by barbed wire so rusty that the Arab children could reach up and grind it to red dust between finger and thumb. Then spit on the sand inside.

The peeling white gates had been wired up, by order of the Flossies. Nobody dared go in, even if they wanted to. Only balls of rolling desert weed ran through, caught on the arms of the leaning white crosses, then blew away back to the desert. Rags of Arabic newspaper caught and fluttered like dying birds on the wire. And in the morning the windswept sand was scribbled with the tracks of sandsnakes, passing in the night.

Major Wood's cross leaned less than most. The newest and last. Beneath, Major Wood slept on with honor. He had not heard; was not disturbed.

Whatever stirred in answer to his son was much nearer home.

Next morning, early, Simon went back to the turnip field. The sun was above the horizon, but mist was still down. A golden mist, that somehow seemed to hang more solidly in the hedgerows. Curving shapes draped from branch to branch, making individual trees look like huge golden ghosts. He laughed; the curving shapes were only cobwebs,

cobwebs spun in the night and thick with dew; strings of pearls, and the rising sun shone inside every pearl. And more webs were spun between the turnips in their rows; each row looked like a moving wave of a glittering sea stretching nearly to the horizon. The roof of the mill was very faint in the mist, like an island in that golden sea. . . . He looked higher, and the rising sun blinded him, even through the mist.

He soon tired of it; but still hung about, feeling that he'd left something at the gate overnight that he shouldn't. Almost expecting to find a sodden kite or a newly rusted air pistol.

And then it came to him.

The mill lay directly beneath the rising sun. East-by-south.

When he had called to his father last night, he had been directly facing the mill . . . might have been talking to the mill.

Now, too late, he remembered smelling the dank smell; the smell of the mill pond. It worried him. He had only meant to talk to his father, as he often had. He resented the idea of the mill being between them. It was another . . . intrusion.

Rubbish. But the thought stuck in his mind like a fish-hook. He suddenly realized he didn't like the mill much any more. In fact he very much disliked it. He wished he hadn't sat at that wooden table, on that wooden chair, playing with the old bitten pipe.

He decided he wouldn't go to the mill again. It was a horrible gloomy place. He would stay at home more; play with Jane, help Mum. . . . Then he remembered last night, and the awful thing he had done to Mum. He was cut off. He was cut off from Mum, and cut off from Jane. Jane had said, I hate you. But she hadn't meant it. It would all blow over. . . . But Mum had said she would send for someone who would deal with him. Who? A doctor? The yellow van to take him away? Dark consulting rooms with horrible middle-aged bald men with waistcoats and foreign accents, who watched you like cats and asked you why you'd said or done what you had said and done without thinking?

Or Nunk? If Nunk came, it would be worst of all. Nunk loved Mum. Nunk had standards of behavior. Which didn't cover using Father's uniform to make Mum unhappy.

Run, Simon, run for cover. Run back to what you know before it's too late—if it's not too late already. Even Joe Moreton seemed bearable this morning.

As he turned to go, he took one last look across the field to the mill. The sun had risen a little more; it did not get in his eyes so much. Then he peered more closely. For he had the stupid illusion that there were three people standing in front of the mill; knee-deep in turnips, as if they were wading through the green gold sea. . . .

Then the sun blinded him again. Silly fool, he thought, and ran indoors to have breakfast. There was bacon frying, and Jane playing on the floor, illegally in her pajamas, getting her knees filthy and being nagged as usual. And Joe warming his backside against the Aga, and the kittens feeding in a purring mass, and Mum in her turquoise dressing gown. All safe and usual.

Then Jane looked up at him; and her face was the face of a suspicious stranger.

"Hallo, Jane."

She looked down at the floor again, quickly; and Mum did not tell her to say hallo either. Mum kept her head down over the stove, looking pale and ill. And Joe held his first cup of coffee and stared blankly out of the kitchen window at nothing.

The silence grew and grew; nobody looking at him. It was like still being outside, alone with the mill and the idea that there were three people wading through the turnips toward the house. . . .

"Hallo, Mum," he said, as brightly as he could.

"Hallo, Simon," she said automatically; a push-away hallo.

"Hallo, Joe."

"Hallo," said Joe, carefully neutral, still staring out of the window. Then he turned to Mum and said, "How long will breakfast be?" though he could see bloody well that the bacon and eggs were nearly cooked.

Simon bent down to stroke the cat and kittens. And they stopped purring.

He *was* outside. Outside the family.

Alone with the mill.

Joe ate quickly, as if he hadn't eaten for a week, and went whizzing up to his studio even before he'd finished his second cup of coffee. He took the coffee with him in his hand. Jane just vanished. Mum, with a sigh, began washing up.

"Shall I dry for you?" Simon asked.

"If you like," she said, listlessly, not caring if he did or not.

They washed and dried up in silence.

"Right," said Mum. "I must go and do the beds."

Everyone was leaving him; no one could stand him being near. It terrified him.

"Mum?" He wanted to say he was sorry. But when she looked at him, he knew it wouldn't be any good. She'd just brush it off like a fly.

"What?" she said, like she couldn't bear him speaking to her.

So he didn't try. Instead he said, "Can I borrow your binoculars? The bird-watching ones?"

"Yes," she said, tightly. "But just make sure nothing happens to them, will you?"

"What do you mean?"

"You know very well what I mean. Don't drop them in the fish pond or anything. It would be just *too* boring, Simon."

"I wouldn't *do* that."

"Wouldn't you?" Her eyes were blank. "All right, then."

He took the binoculars down to the turnip field gate; got them into focus. He wanted to prove that there was really nothing in the field by the mill; that his stupid eyes were playing him tricks. It was so distant. . . .

But his eyes weren't playing him tricks.

There were three figures standing among the turnips. Quite motionless. So inhumanly motionless it was beyond belief. Staring at the house. Who *were* they? He focused and refocused frantically for a better view. He *had* to know.

Then he laughed. They were only scarecrows. Two male, one female. The front male was big and burly. The female stood beside him, just on his right. The other male was much further back.

111

As he watched, the woman raised an arm, and pointed. But it was only the wind. For he could see the little gust silvering the turnip leaves too. Her arm was only an empty rag, that the wind would blow easily.

Stop being stupid, he told himself. The farmer had made the scarecrows simply to scare away the crows.

Did crows *eat* turnips? Enough to be a nuisance? Crows ate dead animals, surely—rabbits flattened by traffic on the road. He had often seen them flying away as the Morris approached. Sometimes they flew away too late, and the car flattened them, to a nasty flutter of black feathers . . . which other crows. . . .

Mr. Mercyfull said crows attacked living lambs, in the lambing season.

Mr. Mercyfull hated crows more than anything.

Mr. Mercyfull said crows could tell whether you were carrying a shotgun or not. That they could even tell a shotgun from a stick. If you pointed a stick at them, they ignored it. If you pointed a shotgun, they were off like the clappers. They could even swerve at right angles if you shot at them in mid-air. Crows could count humans, up to the number of five. Or so Mr. Mercyfull said.

Anyway, there wasn't a crow in sight. Come to that, there wasn't any bird in sight, over the whole great prairie of the field. He searched carefully with the binoculars. Not a sparrow in the hedgerow even. Only a kestrel hovering, far away, beyond the village in the opposite direction. So, O.K. That meant the scarecrows were working. That was what they were for, wasn't it? Be no point to making them, otherwise.

Only the guy who'd made them certainly knew how to

make them lifelike, even if their arms were no more than rags. Then he thought, maybe the guy *made* the woman's arm just a rag, so it would blow in the wind and scare the crows. He'd be some old local; probably some old gaffer with sixty years of skill behind him. He'd like to meet him.

It was just that—the scarecrows seemed oddly . . . familiar, somehow. He couldn't tell why.

That was daft. He returned the binoculars to Mum, putting them back into their case with much more care than usual. "Told you I wouldn't damage them, old silly."

"Yes, Simon," she said, in a carefully meaningless tone. "If you want to do something useful, go down to Cosima's for a loaf, will you?"

Anything to be rid of him.

13

COSIMA WAS THE ONLY FRIEND Simon had made in the whole village. A lively lady, with elegant legs that you saw too much of, because she still clung to short skirts and bicycled round the village on breezy days. She often gave you a shock, being partial to wigs so that she seldom looked the same two days running. She had a long blonde wig, which she put on just before she closed the shop to go out for the evening, which made her look as sexy as Marlene Dietrich. Only when she was too busy, she wore her own hair, which was short and bubble-cut.

Things *happened* to Cosima. But she never told you all at once; they were more like telly serials, though they made *Crossroads* seem *very* dull. Once, she'd smelled a terrible smell of gas in the middle of the night. Next day the Gas Board had come and ripped up every floorboard, especially under her newly laid wall-to-wall carpet, which cost two hundred pound cut-price in Macclesfield. Nevertheless, she was lost in admiration at the Gas Board's devotion to duty. Next day, they returned, with the Inspector. Who pronounced himself Baffled. Though he obviously Knew What He Was Doing. Finally, at the last possible moment, the leak had been found in the least accessible place. Disaster averted by a whisker . . . only that had been the day the Nasty Great Thing had run over Cosima's hand as she opened a bag of Cyprus potatoes, and vanished behind the deep freeze. The Police had been called; fetched a man from Manchester University who had shown Cosima a huge colored book of Nasty Great Things. Cosima had picked one out which turned out to be an Egyptian spider scorpion; any bite of which would be instantly fatal. Four policemen with special gloves ransacked the shop, raping open boxes of catfood and apples; looting the jumbled treasure of years. The spider scorpion evaded capture. The man from Manchester said it Could Be Anywhere, and might live a month. The whole shop took on the air of the Battle of Britain, and Cosima wore wellies and elegant purple elbow-length gloves day and night. She named the scorpion Percy and looked hourly for his re-appearance. At the end of the month, Percy was discovered with his legs turned up, stone dead, under a stack of Choice Pineapple Bits. There was great rejoicing, and the man from Manchester was summoned again. Only to find that Cosima had interred Percy in her garden, under a cross made of two wooden lolly sticks. Cosima grieved for Percy; dead so far from home

114

and kin on sunny Cyprus. The man from Manchester took him away unfeelingly in a jar . . . but just then, a pattern of cracks appeared in Cosima's bedroom ceiling, directly over her bed. Looking like a map of South America. . . .

But Cosima had time for other people's troubles, even in the midst of her own. Her pretty clown-face would turn utterly tragic at accounts of crucifixion by lumbago, or the iniquities of the Social Security. She *Felt*. Only, Simon noticed that once the person she'd Felt for had gone, she would whisk briskly around her shelves with a pink feathery dusty-on-a-stick, humming selections from *Oklahoma*. Probably to take her mind off the world's woe.

Mind you, when something really needed doing, like an old bereaved pensioner living alone, Cosima saw to it. Clothes were laundered, homemade pies delivered. Cosima had minions everywhere. And news. . . . Who needed Radio Manchester when they had Cosima? You couldn't see in her shop windows, because they were plastered with HOMES WANTED FOR TWO ADORABLE BLACK KITTENS between BEST BRITISH SHERRY BRING YOUR OWN BOTTLE and CARRYCOT FOR SALE BLUE AS NEW £2.

And she let you take a long time spending your tenpence, mauling over the rack of wrapped chocolate bars. And told you what news was fit for your ears. Only, Simon always got out of the shop quickly when somebody else came in, because Cosima was liable to draw attention to his beautiful manners, so unlike most kids these days, and all due to a Public College education and Breeding showed. . . .

Cosima had a dark, solid husband called Ernest, who only appeared at closing time, smoking a pipe, making sure Cosima closed when she was supposed to close. But until that moment, he would stand at the back of the shop in utter contentment; with the air of a man contemplating his prize-winning marrow or acknowledging with slight nods an excellent inning at Old Trafford.

Simon parked his bike and slid into the shop through the open door. Cosima was just winding up one of her quieter monologues called "They can do wonders with arthritis these days." Simon lurked behind the rack of fruit pies, in case she did an encore on Public Colleges; until the other woman departed.

"And how's His Lordship today?" asked Cosima, who didn't miss much. "*You* don't like fruit pies. I once knew a man who worked making them . . . what he told me, I'd never eat another . . . not till my dying day."

Simon didn't ask why she cheerfully sold them. Instead, he said, "Is there some old man makes scarecrows round here, Mrs. Brown?"

Cosima considered, head on one side. "Not that I ever heard of. You can buy cardboard ones in the gardening shops. Made by Fison's Seeds or something. I remember scarecrows when I was a lass . . . but not round here. Why?"

"Someone's put up three in the field behind our house. Who owns the field?"

"Used to be old Mr. Timpson's . . . lovely little farm he had—cows. Then he got past it, and his lad went off to be an atomic scientist, so he sold it to some big city syndicate. And they pulled out all the hedges and made it one big nasty field. We never see them—they don't bother. Just send fellers with machines a few times a year, and *they're* contractor's men. They had an airplane here, this spring, zoom-

116

ing about like a Spitfire, putting out that insecticide till you could choke like poison gas. Mr. Bellows had just painted his house cream and maroon, and it turned all gray all over, and he took them to court and they had to pay up four hundred pound compensation . . . but even then they never come to see, just sent a lawyer feller. They just don't care about us . . . and that field gets so full of weeds it would break old Mr. Timpson's heart, only he went to live with his daughter in Plumley and didn't have to watch, thank God. . . ."

"Scarecrows?" asked Simon politely.

Cosima frowned. You could see she didn't like anything happening in the village she didn't know about. "It's the wrong time for scarecrows. You should put them up when the seeds are planted, or the plants are little and tender. I'll ask. . . ."

He chose a small bar of chocolate for himself, grabbed a loaf, paid, and went.

Back in the garden, he tried to find something to do. But he could sort of feel the scarecrows watching him, even through the hedge. He kept on peeping through, to see what they were up to. They didn't seem to have moved. But why should he expect them to move? Except that arm waving on the woman, like beckoning, every time the wind blew. . . .

Why *were* they so familiar?

In the end, his own stupidity infuriated him. He began sweating, and though he took his pullover off, he didn't stop sweating. The sun was bright, but was it really all that hot?

He remembered Father's voice. "Head straight for what you're scared of, Simon. It'll usually run away, if you do. If not, you're no worse off."

So he went, across the turnips. The bruised track they'd made the day they rescued the kittens had almost healed; you could hardly see it, but for some reason he stuck to it. There seemed to be a shallow depression in the ground there, as if there'd once been a path, a right of way, before the syndicate ripped the whole farm into one great field. The path seemed to grip his feet, like a railway line grips the wheels of an engine. It seemed the right place to walk. He was careful where he stepped, in case the vicar was watching.

Halfway across, he shivered. Felt spooky. Stupid, feeling spooky in blazing sunlight. But the field was so big, and so empty, and when he looked back, Mill House seemed very far away. He spun round looking for some other human being, but there was no sign of anyone, all the way to the circular horizon. A car passing on the road made him feel better, but when its noise faded, that made him feel worse again. He had to force himself to go on.

The scarecrows watched him come. The first one was *very* big. Bulky in an old blue gaberdine, tied round the middle with string. He had a broad, cocky face, with a beard made of frayed hempen rope, that blew in the wind when the woman's arm rose and fell. He had a rolled bala-clava helmet on his head, and a stick in one hand, and his other arm round the shoulders of the woman. He looked bullying, and yet somehow not very sure that his bullying would work. A bit like old Bowdon, after Simon had hit him. Bowdon after the bathroom. . . .

The woman was facing sideways. Her woman's coat was tied round with string as well, but the arm that lifted and beckoned was pure white rag; so tattered with age and wind it looked like lace. It had no hand on the end.

118

She was looking not at the man, but over the man's shoulder; at the second man, who was standing a long way behind. At least . . . not standing, but almost like he was walking up behind the big man, with a stick in his hand too. His head was tipped, facing down at the ground; his cap was pulled well down over where his eyes should have been. He had no face at all, just shadows in damp straw; but you could make a face out of the shadows. Only, each time you looked, the face was different. Somehow, you could tell he was up to no good. And you could tell that the big man didn't know he was there. But the woman did. She was waiting for him to come up behind the big man and . . . what . . . ?

Ten yards away, Simon stopped. He couldn't make himself go any further, try though he might. Instead, he walked round them; thinking that from behind, the sticks and things that held them up would make them look fake; like behind the scenery at the school play, where it was all paint brushes and bits of rope and people's scripts. But the scarecrows looked just as real from the back. The guy who made them certainly knew what he was doing. A real artist. Joe Moreton would be interested . . . but Simon blocked Joe Moreton from his mind. He didn't want to owe anything to Moreton.

In fact, the scarecrows were worse from behind. They stood between him and the house. And from the hunch of the second man's shoulders, Simon just knew he was going to do something horrible to the first man.

And the woman knew. She wanted him to. . . .

Oh, rubbish. He stared around for anything that would help. A vapor trail from Manchester Airport in the clear blue sky; the noise of a tractor. . . .

119

Nothing. Just turnips and silence. Then he thought that if he tried to run away back home, the rows of turnips would make it very difficult. They would catch at his feet and trip him. Slow him down; tripping and falling. With the scarecrows following. He was sweating like a pig now. The sunlight made it worse when it should have made it better. . . .

He ran round quickly to the front of the scarecrows again.

The woman's arm raised and beckoned. Had there been a gust of wind that time? He hadn't felt one. *Why* did they look so familiar?

And then . . . he knew.

The blue gaberdine, the rolled balaclava helmet. . . .

The scarecrows were wearing the clothes from the mill. The clothes he had tried on.

Someone had made them, using the old clothes from the mill. . . .

A rage seized him. He flew at the first two scarecrows. Pushed them with all his might. Rocking, they resisted; he could feel the weight of the earth, of the field, around their sticks. Then the earth cracked, the red earth, and they fell together with a soft rustling and crackling, the man on top of the woman.

They looked like victims in a road accident, or on a telly news from Northern Ireland. No, they didn't. They still looked alive and well. Like they were . . . making disgusting animal noises; in the middle of the day, in the middle of a field, in broad view of everybody.

He turned on the third scarecrow; advanced. But he still couldn't read the third scarecrow's look. The third scarecrow was far, far worse. The third scarecrow looked like he might fight back. . . .

Simon got to within a yard; then a dank musty smell hit him; like the smell from the mill pool. Maybe it *was* the smell from the mill pool.

He turned and ran. The leaves of the turnips did catch and whip at his ankles. He did fall and get up, looking over his shoulder.

The scarecrows hadn't moved. The third one still looked ready, threatening. The other two still lay in each other's arms, obscene, even more convincing now they were partly hidden. The man's back was humped, the woman's arm outstretched. And her head was still turned, so she could watch the third one come. And the first man still hadn't noticed.

Simon regained the gate to the garden, panting and slobbering and shaking all over.

Deep down, he knew there had been a fight; and the scarecrows had won.

14

HE STUMBLED into the kitchen. The Aga was turned down low, but the warmth against his backside was a comfort; in spite of the heat of the day, he felt cold and shivery again. The smells were good too: cakes baked, the sharp clean smell from the vegetable rack. The electric clock hummed and clicked soothingly, and he felt a bit better.

There was a scurry from the cardboard box, and a kitten skittered across the floor, braked hard with its front legs, was overtaken by its back legs, and ended lying in a heap facing the way it had come. Another kitten emerged from the shadows and pounced on it gleefully. There was a fierce whirr of legs, and the pair vanished again, heading in opposite directions.

Those two were fine, if raising more and more hell every day meant they were fine; though still too leggy and thin. Mother-cat was fine too. The amounts of food she ate were a daily wonder. Simon looked into the box. Mother-cat was out ratting; only the third kitten remained. It, too, was better. The terrible crusts of green filth had stopped oozing from its eyes. Mum no longer had to bathe them three times a day. The eyelids were pink and normal now. But still tight shut, like a newborn kitten's. It sometimes got up on its wavering legs and wandered round the box, bumping into things over and over. It was doing that now.

He watched it with despair. The bigger and stronger it got, the more it would simply bump into things—the blind cats he'd known were old cats, who had gone blind slowly, so they could get used to it. They were slow anyway, and no longer went anywhere, except a well-worn triangle between a dish of food, a place by the fire and a quick nip outside to relieve themselves; they were O.K. till they died. But young cats wanted to jump and leap and play—and the other kittens bullied the blind one. Nipping it as they nipped each other, and it would try to retaliate and not know how. Some day he knew he would have to let it go to the vet's and be put to sleep. But Mum would wait till he gave the word. That was the awful thing.

He picked up the kitten; it gave a squeak of terror. It always did. The others didn't. It swung its head blindly from left to right and left again. Frantic. He held the head still. Made himself look at the hopeless-closed eyes.

One eye opened. Not completely; only a tiny triangle of black in the middle of the stuck-together pink eyelid. But as he turned its head to the light of the window, the little triangle glistened healthily. There was nothing nasty behind *that* eyelid. And the other eye was starting to open too.

Choked with hope, he whizzed a finger past the kitten's face. It gave a flick, as if following the finger . . . but it could have been coincidence. He did it again. And again the kitten seemed to follow. A third time, it didn't. But a fourth time it did. . . .

He became aware he was being watched by someone standing in the open door that led to the dining room. Someone big and very silent. Someone who had been watching him for some time.

He whirled.

It was Joe Moreton. A look was fading from Joe Moreton's face, as if Joe Moreton was ashamed of it. But it hadn't been a look of hate or spite; Simon knew all about hate and spite. Sadness? Regret? He didn't know. But it hadn't been hate, and it was gone now anyway. Replaced by a look of careful don't-give-two-buggers.

"It can see. I think it can see," said Simon.

"I know," said Joe Moreton. "I thought so too."

"Why didn't you tell me?"

"I didn't want to build your hopes up. It still mightn't be true. But I *think* it is."

Somehow Simon knew that Joe Moreton had been picking up the kitten twice a day and looking at it too.

"Hey, they're *my* cats!"

123

"Yeah," said Joe Moreton. "Your cats. But there's no charge for looking."

"I don't mind," said Simon. Then put the kitten back abruptly, because he was blushing.

"What you going to do with them?" asked Joe Moreton.

"Keep them. *All*."

"O.K."

"I'll pay you for their keep."

"O.K."

"How much do they cost?"

"Dunno. You'll have to ask your mother."

"I suppose . . . I could find good homes for a couple —those two." He pointed to the two frenzied battling bodies. "When they're bigger."

"You could put a notice in Cosima's window."

"Yeah."

"Want a cup of coffee?" asked Joe Moreton, going with the kettle toward the sink.

"Don't mind."

"How many sugars?"

"Two."

He even said "Thanks," when Joe gave him the cup and ambled back to his studio. Joe would tell Mum, and Jane would pick it up, and soon there would be the start of peace. He felt safe—till he went back in the late afternoon to look at the scarecrows again.

Someone had put the two he'd knocked over back on their feet.

Next morning, they were still in the same place.

Well, why the hell shouldn't they still be in the same

place? What did he expect them to do—walk about? Nevertheless, he was nervous enough to be at Cosima's the moment her shop opened.

But there was nothing about scarecrows on Cosima's early newscast. A two-headed lamb had been born out of season at Goostrey; for which Cosima blamed them atomic buggers at Windscale and they would blow us all up sooner or later. Old Mr. Farthing was a lump better, but Mrs. Leach was worse. And the price of bacon wholesale was now beyond belief. . . .

Simon had a better idea. Mr. Mercyfull would know.

As life would have it, Mr. Mercyfull was late. It was nearly eleven, and Simon near despair, before he heard:

When I-hi survey the wondrous cross
On which the Prince of Glory died
My richest gain I count but loss
And pour contempt on or-hor-horll my pride.

Mr. Mercyfull had a large piece of elastoplast among his white skinhead hair. "Had one o' me queer do's. I had a terrible head all neet an' I were just cleaning out grate for me dowter an' I came ower dizzy and banged me head on corner o't'mantelpiece. Came to me senses lyin' in t'ashes, wi' a greet lump knocked out o' marble fireplace. But ye know what? Me headache were clean gone. So I knows how t'cure it next time it comes on—I'll just put down me head an' run street into t'fireplace. . . ." He sat down unusually quickly in his wheelbarrow, and took out his orange device.

"Mr. Mercyfull—what's that roof we can see across the field?"

125

Mercyfull gave him an old-fashioned look and said, "Ye know damn well what yon is—the mill. But I'll tell ye something for nothing. See that roof—it's t'same as the one on your house. Yon's mill, and this is Mill House, an' they were built at same time, hunnerds o' years ago. Millers liked living in t'village, but they had to have mill near t'watter."

"Did you know any millers?"

"I knowed two millers—old miller and young miller. Old miller was a hard man—left a fo'tune. Ye shoulda seen 'im shekking sacks to get last few grains out—even when he owned half t'village. He was past eighty when he died —ower a quarrel about handful o' grain—dropped down dead in millyard wi' t'grain in his hand." Mr. Mercyfull said this with great approval, as if the old miller had won the Nobel Prize for Stinginess. "Old miller were into everythin'—cartin' and hosses—that's how I knowed him— buyin' and rentin' houses—never replaced a brokken pane o' glass, no matter how much tenants complained. He cut up for a tidy sum when his will were read.

"But young miller were soft. I went te school wi' him. All t'lads knocked lumps off him, till he run home blabbin'. Nob but a greet soft lump all his life. His da had him runnin' day and neet; he would send him down village for an ounce o' baccy, even when he was forty year old. Young miller were forty-five when his da died. His da left him every penny, 'cause he hated him less than he hated onybody else. Money went to t'young miller's head—'cause he'd worked for his da all his life and only got ten shillin' a week pocket money. Grand ideas young miller had— spent money like watter in t'pub, tryin' te buy friends. . . .

126

"An' there were a lass in village—Josie Cragg—a right looker, bit o' gypsy, dark an' flashy. All t'lads were after her—fancied her meself—she'd have needed tekkin' in hand, mind—but she wuddent look at the likes o' me. Any road, young miller set his sights on her, and she married him for his money, in spite of his age. She bore him two childer—a boy an' a girl.

"Then Second War came, and miller lost his taste for running t'mill—had a bellyful when his da were alive. An' he were too busy smarming his way into War Ag committees and ARP committees. By gi'ing councillors whisky an' runnin' a grand big car on Black Market petrol. So he got in a feller called Ray Starkey to run t'mill. Silent kind o' man; hardly gie ye the time o' day. I reckoned he was a deserter from t'Army, though *he* reckoned he was fra Liverpool and couldn't get into t'Army on account o' various veins. Still, he ran t'mill well enough—mainly coarse feedin' stuff for cattle. Mill shoulda closed down years afore, only being wartime, and with so many mouths to feed, they kep' it goin'. . . .

"Onyway, it soon became obvious to everyone 'cept young miller that Starkey were robbin' him blind. One bag in ten, they reckoned. Folk tried tellin' miller, but he were never one to listen. Him an' his high-and-mighty ideas— thowt no one could put onything ower *him*. An' flour weren't all Starkey were gettin'. Josie Cragg—Josie Cragg as was, I mean—was always droppin' ower to t'mill to see how things was goin'. An' soon things were goin' very well —for Josie an' Starkey, if ye know what I mean?" Mr. Mercyfull caught Simon's eye and laughed; that knowing, crowing laugh that Simon hated.

127

"Again, folk tried tellin' miller, but he wuddent listen. Far too grand te admit that onything like that could happen to him. But he started drinkin' heavier, any road. Then one night in t'pub, when he were drunk as a lord, it seemed to sink home te him. He went off in his grand car—a Wolseley, a Wolseley Ten it was. Weaving up t'village street from side te side like he were River Weaver itself. Goin' ter have it out wi' Starkey. Lads were all for goin' wi' him, 'cause a lot had it in for Starkey, an' a lot had been keen on Josie Cragg. But miller was too big to want any help.

"He was never seen again—not alive, any road. An' those who seen him after wished they hadn't."

Maddeningly, he paused and looked down at his little orange contraption, which he had been turning and turning with his great hands as he spoke. He pressed a lever, and a spoiled mess of tobacco and shredded paper spilled out. "Beggar it," he said, and maddeningly started the whole tedious process all over again. Then he had to get the pathetic fag alight, and it took five matches. "I don't know as I owt to tell ye t'rest," he added, thoughtfully.

"It's a bit late for that," said Simon, because an awful unease was pulling at his guts. "I can ask anybody now."

"So ye can," said Mr. Mercyfull, as if that relieved him of all responsibility. "Onyway, next morning, Tom Herdwick took ower a load o' grain for millin', an' Starkey refused to do business wi' him, flat. Mill were brokken. Tom Herdwick, he was pushed for time; he were all for goin' into t'mill to see what were brokken, but Starkey just shoved him out on t'door, very nasty. Herdwick dropped a word to millwright ower Mobberly way. But Starkey wouldn't let millwright in either. Slammed an' barred door in his face.

"That caused talk. Specially as miller weren't seen for a week, nor his grand car neither. Someone went ower to Knutsford an' had word wi' poliss.

"Josie an' Starkey told same story. Young miller had gone for Starkey an' lost t'fight an' driven off in a drunken rage an' they hadn't neither on 'em seen hide nor hair of him since.

"Onyway, it looked black for them. Polisses turned mill upside down, an' all t'fields around. Dragged ponds and mill pool wi' great long irons till they were sick, and found nowt. Then one or two folk remembered hearing a car go through t'village at two in t'morning, very unsteady an' heading up t'Manchester Road. Then the polisses in Manchester found the car—what was left on't—on a bombsite i' Withenshaw. Black marketers had tekken all t'wheels an' left it propped up on bricks. Tekken engine, too, an' all dials, and kids had smashed t'headlights. Only number-plates was left.

"Then it all seemed to blow over. Josie an' Starkey took to coming down pub together, spendin' money like there was no tomorrow. Folk gossiped; but they didn't do nowt, 'cause Starkey were a hard bitter man, and nobody had cared much for young miller.

"Only thing was, people needed use on t'mill and Starkey still reckoned it wouldn't wok. So farmers complained to t'Ministry, and Ministry made a possession-order. They could tek your farm from under your feet in them days, if they reckoned ye weren't runnin' it right. One morning early they came wi' a load o' officials, an' a millwright and a couple o' polisses, in case Starkey turned nasty—two whole carloads there was.

"But there was nobody about. They brok the little win-

129

dow in t'door an' eased latch up. There was Starkey's coat hanging on t'wall an' his pipe on t'table, still warm. Like he'd seen 'em coming across t'fields an' run. Millwright checked mill workings an' found nowt wrong wi' 'em . . . so he opened sluice. There was a greet groaning from t'big wheel, but nowt moved, and water began spewing out all ower t'mill, and wheel sounding fit to crack.

"Then wheel turned; and up came young miller three weeks dead. Jammed in t'wheel he was, an' went round three times more afore they stopped it. The man from t'Ministry, he were took bad wi' his nerves an' were in Winwick Hospital for nigh a year, and even t'poliss was sick. . . .

"Then they went down t'village, to this very house, te see Josie Cragg, an' she came out o' yon door in her nightie. An' when they told her, she didn't shed a tear, only asked where Starkey was.

"But when they told her Starkey were gone, she shed enough tears then, and told a right yarn. How young miller had gone for Starkey, and Starkey pushed him down t'mill race on purpose while it were wokkin'.

"So they asked her why she hadn't sent for poliss, an' she said she was afear'd o' Starkey. Which seemed a bit odd, since she hadn't stopped slippin' up to t'mill to see to Starkey's welfare most nights. But they let her go, temporary-like, an' she might ha' got away wi' it, for Starkey was known to be a bad 'un, and women do queer things when they're smit on a man. . . .

"Only Royal Navy caught up wi' Starkey. He'd signed on at Liverpool, on a boat bound for New Zealand. Navy flew him back from a place called Sierra-all-alone. An' when Starkey heard what Josie had told t'poliss, he blabbed everything. How Josie had been on at him for months, day an' neet to do in t'miller. An' she would marry him, an' he could have all t'miller's money.

"I went up to t'Knutsford Assizes, when they were browt to trial. They could neither on 'em think of owt, in t'witness box, 'cept gettin' one another hanged. An' they managed that, both of 'em. Him at Strangeways in Manchester, an' her at Holloway in London.

"And nobody's really used t'mill from that day to this. The Ministry tried puttin' hired men in, one after t'other. Browt fellers from as far off as Bristol. But the moment someone told 'em about them two mekkin free wi' each other, while t'miller lay at bottom o' t'mill race under their very bed . . . nobody would stay. Couldn't pack their bags fast enough. . . ."

"What happened to the children?" breathed Simon.

"Oh, the lad—he were very wild. Brok his neck ridin' t'hoss when he were fotteen. An' the little girl just pined away, they reckon."

Simon went quickly to the toilet and was sick. He spent the rest of the day in the kitchen, sitting by the Aga to keep warm, trying to read *Watership Down*. The cat helped a bit; when he took her on his knee she still purred, but she soon wanted to get down. The kittens helped a bit too, skittering around his feet with their crazy games. Even the once-blind kitten now, its eyes nearly wide open. Though it was not as good as the others at running and frequently squeaked as it got knocked down and bitten.

Joe Moreton came in several times; and every time he did, he tried to talk to Simon. About the weather, or the picture he was trying to paint, or about the book on Simon's knee. But it all seemed unreal, like a bad, boring telly program that Simon didn't really want to watch.

Only Mum seemed real, and she was narky. Wanting him out of the kitchen; asking why he didn't get out and play in the sunshine.

But he knew what was waiting for him outside in the sunshine. Sooner or later, he would have to go and look over the gate, over the turnip field. And Starkey and Josie Cragg and the young miller would be there, watching him. And somehow he knew they would be nearer. Coming along the sunken path under the turnips; the path they had trod—the path all the millers had trod for hundreds of years since mill and mill house were built.

Once, in a panic, he followed Mum to her bedroom, wanting to tell her everything. But at the bedroom door she turned on him and said, "For God's sake, Simon, stop following me about like a bloody shadow. You're getting on my nerves. Are you *ill* or something? If you're not, you soon will be, mooning around the house like this. Now, stop it, and go and play, or I'll take you to the doctor. Are you trying to drive us all mad or something?"

There was a desperation in her voice he'd never heard there before. He knew that if he told her the truth, she wouldn't believe him. It would just seem the latest of his bloody silly tricks. Make things worse. . . .

Joe . . . he thought Joe might understand. But to tell Joe . . . Joe would know *everything* about him, then. Joe Moreton would know he was a coward. He would end up a slobbering heap in Joe Moreton's large arms. Like Jane. Joe Moreton would have him for good. And that wouldn't be fair to Father.

Father, he thought. Father. Father had been lonely like this. Lonely and on his own. But Father had charged the Flossies and killed one; and the other two had ended up under the jeep, screaming their heads off. Father had won; on his own. It was the only way.

Help me, Father.

But he couldn't turn toward east-by-south.

They were in the way, now.

15

HE SAT AT HIS WINDOW, watching. The window glass was old and leaded, and the diamond panes full of whirls and bubbles. He had to have the window open, or he couldn't watch properly. It was pretty cold; an autumn nip in the air. He was wearing three pullovers and an anorak over his pajamas, and he was still cold.

It was moonlight, though. So he could see Them quite clearly. He didn't think They'd moved since dusk. But he couldn't be quite sure, even with the aid of Mum's binoculars. He surveyed Them carefully again. The stupid moon-face of the young miller swam up quite clear. Just a sheet of thick white paper tucked up into the balaclava helmet, with eyes and nose drawn crudely in blue ink, and already smudged with rain. But it held all the miller's uneasy cocky stupidity.

The fringe of rope beard blew in the wind, making him jump. But They *hadn't* moved. They were still behind that extra-high bunch of turnip leaves that looked like a huge rabbit. But he knew they *would* move; if he took his eyes off them for too long. Only if he did his damnedest, he could just hold them at bay.

He yawned; his mind drifted until he was back at school and they were getting changed for a match. Somebody—Hudson—was throwing his boots at people, who were laughing.

The grandfather clock in the hall struck three; and he jolted back awake. He must stay awake. He'd better get up and walk about for a bit. Only he'd better check on Them again first.

They still hadn't moved. So he got up and prowled round the house, easing the stiffness in his bones. Listened at Jane's door; heard her breathing; heard her say something in her sleep, and turn over and breathe steadily again. She was O.K.

Downstairs. He could hear Joe snoring, but had to strain through the boards of the door to hear Mum. It made him feel good. They didn't love him yet; they were still cross with him; but he was keeping them safe.

The kittens were safe too, huddled in their box into an incredibly tight heap that constantly struggled to get tighter and tighter. The mother-cat was out. That worried him. *She* had lived at the mill; did she go back there ratting in the night; up that path, past Them?

He raided the fridge and built a fat cheese sandwich and drank a glass of milk. The milk tasted great, even if it was so cold it made his teeth ache. It didn't matter, with his backside against the Aga. . . .

The bang of the cat flap made him jump. But it was only the mother-cat returning. She rubbed against his legs approvingly and ate the piece of cheese he gave her.

134

If only he had a weapon to use against Them if They came. Something of Father's. But all he had now of Father's was the regimental cap badge that he'd carried in the haversack from Nunk's. And that was already on a string round his neck, under his pajamas. Everything else was in the studio, locked away, ready to go to Nunk. If only. . . .

Then he remembered where Joe kept the studio key: in the inside pocket of his duffle coat. Which was hanging in the hall. He crept along and found it. Then nipped upstairs to have a look at Them again. But They still hadn't moved.

Downstairs again, shivering with triumph now. Into the studio, which smelled not discomfortingly of Joe. The smaller kitbag—yes, there was the long hard lump. He unzipped the bag and slid his hand down the side without disturbing the other clothes, and pulled out Father's webbing belt; with the khaki holster and little ammunition pouches. He drew out the revolver, cold, heavy and oily smelling. It was the old sort—a Webley. Father hadn't used a Browning automatic like the other officers did; like he was supposed to. Father hadn't given a damn for supposed-to. He carried the revolver his own father had carried. Had used—in the First War; in India. Simon was glad. He couldn't have worked a Browning automatic, but he knew how to work this. Father had shown him once. You pressed a little lever and the revolver broke in half, on a hinge at the bottom. Leaving the revolving cylinder looking at you like a face, with six round dark eyes. Simon opened the ammunition pouch (the brass press stud was difficult) and put shiny brass cartridges in five of the round black holes. Not the black hole that lay under the revolver's hammer—that was dangerous—that could make the revolver go off if you

135

dropped it. Father had told him that. He clicked the revolver shut again, put it back in the holster and fastened the belt round his waist. He had to shorten the belt, but Father had shown him how to do that too. When he had finished, the webbing cut into him as he climbed back upstairs; cut into him even through three layers of pullover. But it was a good pain; he felt strong now; magic. Father's revolver would shoot Them full of holes, if They dared come near. Mum's binoculars to watch Them through; Father's revolver to shoot Them with. They hadn't a chance, now . . . and They knew it. They had stayed exactly as They were.

They'd better go back into their rotten mill, and unmake Themselves, if they knew what was good for them. Mill House was safe from Them now, forever.

Comforted, he slept. Head on the open windowsill; one arm lying outside on the dew-dampening roof slates.

"Simon! What in God's name?"

He jolted awake with a start, a terrible pain in the side of his jaw where his head had rested on the windowsill. He looked outside, into a bright sunny morning.

They hadn't moved; indeed (he checked carefully with the rabbit-shaped clump of turnip leaves) they were further away if anything; nearer to the mill.

He turned to her with a smile.

"Hallo, Mum. What's for breakfast?" He felt he could eat a horse.

She began to smile back; then her eyes dropped to his waist.

"What . . . what—where did you get that revolver?

136

That was in Joe's study, locked away. How did you get it. *How?*"

He hung his head and said nothing.

"You stole Joe's key . . . out of his pocket . . . sneaking about in the middle of the night."

He sensed more people in the bedroom doorway. Joe was standing there, looking wary, summoned by the noise. Jane was with him in her pajamas, huddling in close, all eyes, sucking her thumb. As he watched, she reached up and put her other hand in Joe's.

"Give-me-that-thing," said Mum. "Give-me-that-thing-this-minute!"

"No." How could he make her understand? Understand how important it was?

"Give-me-that-thing." Mum's voice rose to the danger-pitch.

"No."

A clout on the side of his face set his head spinning.

"*Give-me-that-thing.*"

"No." He sat down hard on the bed, so she couldn't hit him again.

"Joe," said Mum.

"C'mon, Simon," said Joe, advancing. "C'mon. Don't up-set your mother. Be a good lad. Give it up." His face was wary, but sorry too. And he meant what he said.

"I can't," wailed Simon.

"Don't make me make you," said Joe, sadder than ever. "You'll get it back, I promise. It'll *all* be yours one day. But it's dangerous now, Simon. Be a good lad; give it up—"

"I can't! Don't you see, I *can't.*"

"Take it off him, Joe," said Mum.

137

"I don't want to force him."

"Take it!" yelled Mum. "He's probably got it *loaded*. Is it loaded, Simon?"

"Yes."

"For God's sake!"

Joe reached down for the holster. Simon snatched out the revolver before he could reach it.

"Stand back. Stand back. You can't have it; you can't!"

Infinitely slowly and sadly, Joe reached out to grab his wrist. Simon put his hand behind his back. Joe reached behind his back to take the gun. Began twisting it out of Simon's hand, slowly and gently, but with irresistible force. A force that was making Simon's finger tighten on the trigger.

"Stop, Joe, stop!" he shouted; knowing the danger.

But Joe didn't know the danger. He went on inexorably twisting and shaking the revolver out of Simon's hand.

There was a sharp kick that hurt Simon's wrist, and a terrifying bang inside the little room. A shower of plaster descended from the ceiling, and they all gaped at a huge hole, with ends of worm-eaten boards. While Simon was still staring at the hole, Joe took the gun from him, broke it in half and emptied out the remaining cartridges.

Only then did Mum notice that Joe's hand was bleeding; from a long, straight, red mark across the palm.

"Joe, your hand. . . ."

"It's all right," said Joe, wrapping a hanky round it, which immediately stained red. "I'll just get this thing back to the studio. And I'll give *you* the key this time."

"But it's your *drawing* hand. . . ."

"Try and stop me drawing," said Joe grimly. And went

138

out with Jane, who immediately began telling him, all the way down the corridor, what a *wicked* boy Simon was, and when was the man coming to mend the ceiling and would the rain come into Simon's bedroom and serve him right if it did.

Simon and Mum were left alone. Mum was panting; her nostrils were flared and white. She didn't look like Mum at all, but like his worst enemy.

"Mum." He put out a hand pleadingly.

"You little lunatic. You could have killed Joe. You've probably maimed him for life, so he can never draw again. You little *bastard*."

And then she was hitting him and hitting him, like she would never stop. He took the first few blows in silence, sorry about Joe, feeling he deserved a bashing.

But it went on too long, and then he began to hit back.

They stopped; and glared at each other.

"I saw you born; I saw you come out of my body. But I swear . . . you're no part of me. You're all Wood, Wood, Wood. You're just another one of a long line of. . . ."

But it wasn't what she said. It was the way she said it.

He sat for a long, long time; wondering why he'd ever thought school could be lonely. How much worse could things *get?* There seemed just bottomless pits of worseness. I mean, you could break your leg; or become paralyzed from the waist down; or go blind. Once you started falling into worseness, did you ever stop? Or once you were in it, was it like a whirlpool that sucked you down and down?

Still, you couldn't sit here all day. You had to eat. And something decent might still happen. . . .

139

Or something indecent; like a strange voice in the kitchen. A very loud yakky voice that invaded the staircase every time the kitchen door opened, and threatened to invade the whole house.

He hated strangers at breakfast. He went in the kitchen door with a rush, flooded his cornflakes with milk that bounced off them onto the tablecloth, and plunged into them, head down.

The yakky voice paused, as if weighing him up as a potential audience, then continued.

"I can't get used to doing it, you know. If I do it as long as I live, I shall never get used to doing it. It just doesn't seem right, somehow. Even if I was on the stage fifteen years . . . I started as a girl of sixteen . . . I was innocent . . . I didn't know nothing. My mother didn't like it, I can tell you . . . I think it drove my poor father into his grave. But what I say is, if the talent's in you, you've got to let it out, haven't you?"

Mum was moving about the kitchen, wiping this and that, almost as if she was keeping on the run in case the voice threw something at her. Mum being vague and polite, saying, "Yes, I know," and, "I see how you must feel." It was pretty obvious that this conversation had taken place a lot of times before. Both sides knew all the moves.

"I can't help wondering how *you* must feel about it," said the voice, "being married to him an' all. It just don't seem right. . . ."

"I'm sure you're only doing the job you're paid for, Mrs. Meegan," said Mum, suddenly frosty. "It's just a job like any other."

"Aye, you'd know that," said Mrs. Meegan, "if you'd

lived the life I've lived. All those men's eyes on you. I just turn my mind to higher things. I let tunes run through my head, like Tchaikovsky's Piano Concerto number one. Lovely tune that!" She pronounced it Cheekowski, and began to pom-pom the piano theme; very badly.

Simon stole a quick look at her, past the half-empty toastrack.

She looked artificial. Her hair was a jet, unnatural black, right down to the roots, and so tightly permed it looked like a wig. Her face was so made up, with bright patches of rouge on her cheeks, that she looked like a doll. She wore a black satin-finish raincoat, black shoes and no stockings. And clutched a half-empty black shopping bag on her knees as if she were frightened someone might steal it. It made her knees sag apart, so you could see the fat insides of her thighs.

He looked too long; the woman noticed. As he plunged for a bit of toast, the woman said,

"He your eldest, then?"

"Yes," said Mum.

"Fourteen, is he?"

"Nearly," said Mum.

"Awkward age that. Like our Carrie. Caroline really, but we call her Carrie for short. Carolina Tracy Amantha, to give her her full titles." The woman laughed vulgarly, as if at some obscure joke. "Cheeky they are, at that age. Think they know it all."

The door opened. Joe came in, looked at Simon, then said roughly, embarrassedly, "You ready, Mrs. Meegan?"

"Just let me gather me wits," said Mrs. Meegan, clutching her shopping bag even more tightly, as if all her wits were inside. "Well, it's all in a day's work, I suppose. As the Yanks used to say: another day—another dollar. My, *they* were ones . . . *they* used to keep Warrington lively, till they closed Burtonwood airbase down. Saturday nights—"

"Let's get started," said Joe. "I don't want to waste the light."

Mrs. Meegan departed, swigging her coffee on the hoof. Simon almost felt grateful to Joe.

When the door shut he said, "Is she the char?"

"No," said Mum. "She works . . . for Joe."

"Doing what?"

"In the studio."

"Doing *what?*"

"He's painting her . . . portrait."

"What? With all that make-up She's painted herself already, seems to me." He hoped Mum would laugh; but she didn't. A hideous thought entered Simon's mind. "You don't mean. . . ."

"Yes," said Mum, beating hell out of a saucepan with a scourer. "In the nude. Finish your breakfast. I must get washed up. I haven't got all day."

"Does he paint you in the. . . ."

"No," said Mum. "That's why he's got Mrs. Meegan."

"I think that's disgusting. In *your* house. . . ."

"This is not *my* house. This is Joe's house. And don't start again, Simon. I really couldn't bear you starting again."

He could tell from the sound of her voice that she meant it. He threw down his half-eaten toast and swept out into the garden in a rage. Found a panga in the garden shed. It might have been Father's; then on the other hand it might not. He went and hacked down dock plants at the back of the orchard, till the panga and his hands were green and black with dock blood.

It didn't help at all. The moment he sat down, panting, his eyes went up to the studio window. He wanted to see. He knew it would make him feel awful. But it was there and he had to see it.

There was an apple tree pretty close to the studio window. If he climbed up that. . . .

The trunk was mossy and flaky, and his legs were shaking from hacking the dock leaves. It took him a long time, and he literally had to crawl up the tree on his knees, which was shameful. Once, a rotten branch cracked under his foot and, spreadeagled in the branches, he looked up at the studio window in terror. But nobody noticed; nobody looked out. He settled in a branch and turned.

Mrs. Meegan stood with her back to him, on a wide wooden box on wheels. Although the day was fine, she was surrounded by little electric fires, with black snaky cables running to sockets all over the place. She looked enormous and saggy, with veins on her legs. She was standing with all her weight on one leg, so her hip stuck out like a mountain. She had a hand on that hip and she looked very bored. Probably halfway through Cheekowski's first piano concerto. . . .

Joe was standing on her left, beside a huge white canvas like a sail. His face was screwed up in agony, like an old ugly prune. Kept swinging his head from side to side, from Mrs. Meegan to the canvas; a bit like a spectator at Wimbledon whose favorite player is losing six-nil. He kept holding out his hand with a brush in it; and moving his thumb

143

up and down the brush. He swayed from side to side; stepped back, stepped forward in a ridiculous swaying dance. Every so often, when he stepped back, he bumped into a cupboard and gave himself a fright. Finally, after about five minutes, he stepped up to the canvas and put a tiny cross near the middle of it.

Then he went through the same ridiculous performance all over again; rubbed out the cross he had made with a filthy turpsy rag, and put in another cross about a quarter of an inch to one side.

Simon looked at the canvas. It was nothing like a nudey magazine. It was a maze of small triangles—blue, green, pink, yellow—that seemed to have nothing at all to do with the huge bulges of Mrs. Meegan. Until he looked at Mrs. Meegan again, and saw she *was* sort of funny colored. The backs of her thighs were yellow, like tallow. And her shins were bright pink from the heat of the electric fires. And the fold on her back where her bra strap went was a kind of green. . . .

It was not at all sexy. Simon felt flat as a pancake. He started to climb down; and then Joe saw him.

They stared at each other through the glass. Joe didn't look at all guilty He looked bloody furious, as if someone had jogged his arm when he was writing. He gestured to Simon to get down; as if Simon was a nasty little beetle that had crawled out of a crack in the tree trunk. Simon went on sitting where he was; settled himself quite deliberately. He was *not* a beetle. He had a perfect right to sit in any tree he chose. He was not going to be pushed around any more. He had a right to be *somewhere*.

Joe said something to Mrs. Meegan, and Mrs. Meegan

144

got down off her box, vanished behind a screen, and re-appeared in a maroon silk dressing gown with a fag stuck in the corner of her mouth.

But she didn't look out of the window. She sat down and began massaging the sole of one foot, which was nearly orange in color. Then Joe began showing her something in a magazine. But every so often he would glance across at Simon and make silent furious gestures for Simon to get down.

Then Simon got it.

If Mrs. Meegan knew he was there, she wouldn't half raise a stink. Probably flounce out of the house and never come back. Leaving Joe stuck with a half-finished painting.

Great. Simon went on sitting and glaring. That would teach Joe Moreton what it felt like to be helpless; to have the thing you wanted most in the world torn away from you.

Joe went on wandering around the studio, picking up things and putting them down again in a bigger and bigger tizzy. Mrs. Meegan went on reading the magazine, till her fag burned right down. Then she stubbed it out, and began reluctantly to take off her dressing gown. Her breasts were huge, pendulous and faintly purple. Now she would know who was at the awkward age; cheeky, thinking they knew it all. . . .

But Joe shook his head violently at Mrs. Meegan. She put her dressing gown back on. Joe pointed downstairs and she went.

Victory. Where it hurt most.

Joe picked up a big sketchbook and came to the window. Simon waited for the big, big shouting; the feeble, impotent gestures of rage. Joe Moreton would look ridiculous, like a politician on the telly with the sound turned off. Instead, Joe picked up a pencil and began to draw. Draw Simon. And Joe Moreton's eyes were no longer screwed up in agony; just cool and assured. Like the day he drew the Headmaster. Swiftly, surely, cruelly.

Simon held his position for twenty long shuddering breaths. But all the time he could imagine the savage, scribbled shapes that Joe was putting down. He put out his tongue; put up two fingers, screamed insults. But Joe just drew the tongue, the fingers, the shouting mouth. Joe Moreton making his spider's-web network of lines, and Simon was the poor buzzing fly caught inside them. Joe Moreton was eating him alive. Then he would spit out the bits for other people to laugh at.

Simon leaped from the tree in one wild, reckless leap. Landed in a patch of stinging nettles that old Mercyfull had somehow missed. Must have dropped twelve feet. But he felt the jolt no more than he felt the stinging nettles. He ran for the kitchen door.

Mum looked terrified; Mrs. Meegan, cup in hand, merely startled. Mum caught him by the arm as he started to push past. "Simon! What's the *matter?* Simon!"

"Let me go. He's drawing me! He's *drawing* me!" He ran for the stairs. Mum ran after him. And Mrs. Meegan, cup still in hand. He flung open the studio door.

Joe stepped back from something freshly pinned to the wall. A drawing; of the top of an apple tree. In only a few lines, he had caught its ancient mossy crookedness. And in the crook where a branch met the trunk sat a figure. A figure with its tongue out, and two fingers up, and one

146

leg dangling down the trunk and the other hand resting on the branch. A hunched little figure of pure hate. . . .

"That's *not* me. It's *not*, it's *not*, it's *not!*"

All the adults burst out laughing.

"The spitting image," said Mrs. Meegan. "Mr. Moreton, I take my hat off to you. How'd you do it, sir?"

Simon ran across and pulled the drawing off the wall. The drawing pins spattered on the floor away across the lino. Then he tore the drawing across, and tore it again and again, then dropped the pieces. They lay across the floor and his feet like confetti at a wedding.

"Simon," said Mum. "That picture was worth a hundred pounds."

"I don't care. It was *me*. He stole me."

"It doesn't matter," said Joe Moreton. "He hasn't really torn it up. It's still in my head and he can't tear *that* up." And, very pale, he picked up his sketch pad and began to draw again. The crook of the apple tree.

"*Please*, Joe," whispered Mum. "*Please* don't."

"If it's a lie," said Joe, "it won't hurt him. Lies don't hurt. And if it's the truth, it's about time he knew it."

The little figure with the upraised fingers began to appear again, in the bough of the apple tree; amidst the swift spiderwork of pencil lines.

"*Please*, Joe!" said Mum desperately.

"I've tried to please," said Joe. "And where has it got me? If he wants a fight . . . maybe it's better out than in."

The mouth appeared, a loathsome triangle; and the outstretched tongue.

Simon flung himself on the sketch pad, but Joe was ready. A large hand thumped flat-palmed into Simon's

147

chest, and held him at arm's length while he flailed in-
effectually.

"Children these days," said Mrs. Meegan, slurping her
coffee with gusto. "I don't know what the world's coming
to."

Simon fled. He walked and walked till three in the afternoon. When he got home, Joe Moreton was still painting
Mrs. Meegan. Simon could see the flicker of his blue shirt
through the big studio window.

Mum was waiting in the kitchen. She got up and gave
him his dinner from the oven. There was a glass dish over
it, heavily steamed up, and the food inside was glued to
the red-hot plate with dried-out gravy.

"Simon, I want to talk to you . . ." said Mum.

He listened in silence, prying up bits of meat with the
point of his knife and chewing them without tasting a thing.
In the end he promised not to go near the studio; to stop
provoking Joe; to behave like a civilized human being.

She talked to him very gently; but it was a fake. He
answered very gently, and that was a fake too. It didn't
matter. It was too late anyway.

When he had come home from his walk, he had seen the
scarecrows.

They were halfway across the turnip field.

16

HE CROUCHED BY THE POND in the middle of the garden,
watching the goldfish, the big red goldfish rise and sink
through the muddy green water. They were fat, with smooth

curving sides. Like Mrs. Meegan. Smug. So sure of themselves and their safe muddy world. He could have killed them easy; punctured their smooth sides with one prod of the sharp-snapped stick in his hand.

But he couldn't be bothered. It was too late for that. Too late for anything but to let it happen.

Let *what* happen? He couldn't even begin to guess. Except this morning the scarecrows were nearer; and he could feel them stronger inside his mind. He could feel each one separately now.

The young miller. Thumped at school every day, till he ran home blubbing. To a father who rubbed his face in the dirt even when he was a grown man. Then he got power; money and a big fast car and a pretty wife. He and his wife in the dark, making noises.

But not real power. Trying to buy friends with drinks, and always knowing they were laughing behind his back, even while they were drinking his drinks. And his pretty wife with another man, helping to steal him blind. And then death, down and down in the black water, round and round in the choking mill wheel. And still his wife and the other man, making the animal noises above him, even when he was dead. And still the miller's voice squealed desperately, "I am the greatest." Knowing it was never true.

And he felt Josie Cragg. You've got to have a good time, haven't you? While you're young and still got your looks. You're entitled, aren't you? You got to be free, free from slobby hands groping you every single night. Great fat weight crushing your life out. But all you get's another drunk—and he runs off and leaves you. I'm entitled to more than that. Entitled . . . entitled . . . entitled. . . .

Then Starkey; Starkey was unmentionably worst of all.

149

He fled from Starkey, back to the others. . . .

But all three were hungry . . . to live again. They had lived on their own hate for thirty years, and it was a thin, bitter, unsatisfying thing. Like endlessly drinking vinegar because there was nothing else.

The dead, Simon knew now, were always hungry. And they felt entitled.

They were coming to prey on the fatness of the living. And he, Simon, had opened the larder door and it could never be closed again. Nothing could stop it happening now. He just didn't know how it was going to happen, that's all. He just had to wait.

But it made him jumpy. Like a big storm coming up. He glanced at the sky. There was a film of dirty cloud all over the sky, like thin soup. With patches of failed yellow sunlight like patches of grease floating in the soup. And thicker, darker clouds inside the soup, coming and going like the goldfish in the pond.

Joe Moreton was painting in his studio. No Mrs. Meegan today; the light wasn't right. Joe had the electric light on up there.

Mum was in the kitchen, with both the light and radio on. As if she, too, couldn't bear the approaching silence that closed and closed. The tinny weak voice of the radio just made the silence seem more silent.

Jane was hanging out of her bedroom window. She saw him look at her and called, "Simon, Simon"; voice as irrelevant as a bird's. He didn't bother to answer, or even wave. She was irrelevant. He thought of all the nasty tricks she'd ever pulled; all the tales she'd told. Little blackmailer. . . . But it didn't matter. Only the waiting mattered.

How would it *come?* That was the unbearable bit . . . waiting.

Only the silence, the anger, the hunger, getting worse. Till he felt his head would split.

He heard a bus pull up at the road junction nearby. The throbbing of its engine felt like a terrible impertinence against the silence; like a boy telling a dirty joke in class, when he hasn't heard the Head coming up silently behind him. Get away, bus. This has nothing to do with you. You are blameless, bus. Get away quick, if you know what's good for you.

Obediently, the bus drove off. But now there were feet coming along the road. Impudent feet, silly feet, not caring the danger they were in. Feet that stopped and looked at something; feet that gave a skip of glee. Feet that went with a thin, high, carefree whistle.

The scarecrows' anger grew yet more terrible. Simon hunched close to the ground, rocking, rocking.

"Hallo, you silly sod. What are you up to?" said a voice. A bean-shaped face grinned at him over the front gate. A shock of black hair, sticking up all over the place.

Tris la Chard.

The hate of the scarecrows cracked like a glass bell-jar, shattered. It was like a flash of lightning in his brain. One minute it was there; next minute it was far off. The clouds moved their own separate ways; a bird sang about its business; a little wind blew through the grass. The whole world seemed to get up, shake itself and get on with things. Like an electric train set at the end of a power cut. Simon got up and shook himself too.

"How do you open this bloody gate? People put handles

151

in such daft places." Tris came through, and gave a jump and a wriggle that dumped his rucksack onto the grass. "That thing makes me feel like a carthorse. Pity the humble carthorse. Goldfish?" He crouched by the pond. A goldfish rose and waved its fins, mouthing water. Tris stuck a hand each side of his own head in imitation, and waggled them in pouffish fashion, opening and closing his mouth in rhythm. "Oh, get *off*, honky-tonk!" The goldfish, as if offended, wriggled its tail and vanished. Tris wriggled his hips and said, "I must go and see Everard. Nobody *appreciates* a poor goldfish."

Simon laughed, for the first time in a week.

Mum looked out of the window, waved, and came hurrying across the lawn wiping her hands on a tea towel, all smiles. Her eyes were glowing warm again. Jane waved anew from the window. "Tri-is. Triiiii-iiiiis! Come and *frighten* me. I like it when *you* frighten me."

Summoned by all the racket, Joe emerged, paintbrush in hand.

"How do you do?" said Tris, shaking hands with the paintbrush.

Tris dumped his rucksack on the other bed in the attic.

"Thanks for inviting me. Even if you couldn't be bothered to write yourself. I can just do with a fortnight away from bloody tomato plants. This time of year, Jersey is just one great tomato jungle. To be cleared by yours truly, along with every tramp and layabout on the island. Honestly, there's nothing so depressing as a mile of tomato plants when all the tomatoes have been picked. All yellow and slimy and your hands turn black, and the pong. . . . I haven't been able to face a tomato since I

152

was four. One milligram of tomato sauce gives me the galloping migraines."

Simon saw it all now. Cunning old Mum. Tris was the guy she had got in; the one guy who could deal with Simon.

Simon didn't mind; he would quite like to be dealt with.

Tris burrowed down into his rucksack, strewing clothes all over the place like Vesuvius erupting. Found a pair of leather sandals and put them on. Burrowed again, erupting the rest of the contents, including several transparently greasy paper packets that had been food.

"Got some good cheese," he said. "Camembert. My grandmother gave it me . . . oh." He held up a sock regretfully. "Like a sock-and-Camembert sandwich? It's a *clean* sock."

"No thanks," said Simon. "I'm off socks at the moment —I'm on a diet."

Tris produced a massive air pistol. "Where's the action, squire?" He looked out of Simon's bedroom window, and saw the scarecrows. "Aha—the opposition. The Clancies— the old gunfight at the O.K. Corral." And he had grabbed a tin of pellets, loaded the pistol and disappeared downstairs before Simon could say a word. Through the field gate, and advancing on the scarecrows with the air pistol waggling dangerously loose from the right hip pocket of his jeans, and his arms dangling by his sides, swinging his hips in a bow-legged walk.

"Ah'm coming fo' you, Billy Clancy. Give yo'self up an' there won't be no trouble, boy."

Simon stopped dead in his tracks.

The anger had returned; the sky was suddenly dark and pressing down on his head.

But Tris walked on.

"C'mon, boys. You know it ain't no use getting orkard. There's a nice dry quiet cell, down in the old jail-house. . . ."

The young miller faced up to Tris; fat, stubborn, falsely cocky as ever. The rain had made his face run and dribble even more. But it only made his expression harder to read; more like Starkey's.

"All right, Billy . . . don't blame me . . . just think of your old mother. . . ."

Then Tris crouched, drew and shot all in the same instant. Even as Simon's head began to split open, he had to admit that Tris's act was bloody brilliant.

The pellet took the miller clean between the eyes. The figure swayed slightly, but did not fall.

"So yo' think yo' tough, boy," said Tris. Reloaded and shot; again and again.

Every wound made the miller's face worse.

Then Tris stepped up to the scarecrow, and said, "The trouble with you', boy, is that yo're dead and yo' don't know it." He placed a foot firmly in the miller's chest, and kicked him flat.

Again, the woman fell with the man, as if tied to him; again they fell in an obscene huddle.

"Ah don't hit wimmenfolk," drawled Tris. "Sorry, Ma'am. But yo' shouldn't do that kind of thing. Not in public."

Tris turned to face Starkey. In the act of reloading, he paused. Something about Starkey seemed to get through to him. He mimicked Starkey's pose. Exactly. Then stayed stockstill, as if taking the temperature of the water with his toe.

"I—don't—like—you," said Tris, not in his normal

154

voice. And shot. Again, he was dead accurate. The shot knocked Starkey's cap spinning. Underneath, the packed straw was brown and rotting.

"Eeugh, what a pong!" said Tris. Simon sniffed. The smell of the mill pond. Tris picked up the cap, tried it on his own head, paused again, and looked at Simon.

"For God's sake, Simon, what are you staring at?" Then he threw the cap away among the turnips, and kicked Starkey over in turn. "What else is there round here worth doing?"

"Oho," said Tris. "A path through the turnips. Leading to . . . the Wizard's Castle. The Wizard of Oz. Follow the yellow brick road.

And he broke out into the song from the old movie. *"We're off to see the Wizard, the wonderful Wizard of Oz."* And danced ridiculously, gaily, up the path through the turnips. Just like Judy Garland and the Scarecrow and the Tin Man and the Cowardly Lion.

Simon followed, though his feet dragged through the turnips like lead. There seemed to be a pressure from the mill, radiating outward like a silent, unmoving wind. A wind like a silent, still hurricane, that he had to battle into, like explorers into an arctic blizzard. It was nearly impossible. But Tris was his friend. Tris was good. He couldn't let him go to the mill alone.

It did strike him as funny. Up to this very moment, the mill had tried to suck him in. Like a vacuum cleaner. Now, suddenly, it was trying just as hard to keep him out. That was odd. But the pressure was so terrible on his mind that he just had to concentrate on keeping going.

He caught up Tris by the mill dam. Tris was firing airgun

pellets into the water at a shallow angle; trying to get them to bounce off the water and skim all the way across, like the bouncing-bomb in the Dam Busters. He managed it; one pellet skimmed all the way through a gap in the lily pads to the far shore.

The two ducks appeared round the corner of the island. They were bigger now; but the largest one still swam in front.

"It's de law, boys, beat it!" yelled Tris; and scarpered along the dam wall toward the mill.

Pressure, pressure, pressure. But Simon followed.

Tris sailed through the front door. "What is this place, Simon?"

"I'm not sure."

"Don't tell me you haven't been here before? What you been doing with yourself all these weeks?" They both looked round the room.

The hats and coats were gone off the pegs. . . .

And Simon had a terrible conviction that, back in the turnip field, the scarecrows had got back on their feet, and were facing, now, toward the mill. He and Tris were trapped.

"Not much here . . ." said Tris thoughtfully. "What's all this shredded paper on the table?" He picked up one of the largest pieces. "*Butter ration to be reduced?* Hey, this must be a wartime paper."

"Yeah," said Simon. He had to dredge the answer up from fathoms deep; his voice was a croak.

"Christ!" said Tris. "What's the matter, Simon? You sound like a bloody zombie. I don't think the country air's doing you much good." He peered at Simon in the gloom of the living room. Concerned. "You all right?"

156

For a moment, Simon nearly told him everything. It would have been so easy.

And sounded so potty.

"Got a sore throat," he said. "Had a bit of flu, I think." Tris went on looking at him; not satisfied. Till Simon said abruptly,

"There's a water mill through there. In full working order."

"Great," said Tris. "Let's go." He left his air pistol lying on the wooden table, alongside Starkey's pipe, and made for the door to the interior.

"I'd . . . take that with you, if I were you," said Simon.

"Why? Who'd pinch it? There's been nobody here for years; except you, you crafty old sod." Again he gave Simon an old-fashioned look.

They climbed up through the works of the mill. It was all gallows now; gallows and trapdoors opening under your feet, and ropes in loops and the sack of grain that swung in the draught from the open door behind them; the sack with the frayed strands of rope like flaxen hair.

Simon knew now that Starkey must have had fair hair.

And the footsteps in the flour dust; Mum's, Jane's, his own with the ribbed soles; and the scuffle marks where he had obliterated Joe Moreton's footprints, deliberately, one after the other.

But Tris walked straight across the lot, not giving two buggers.

"You say it's in working order?" he asked incredulously.

"I've had it working," said Simon.

"You've got a nerve," said Tris admiringly. "This whole place is shot to hell. Look at this woodworm—look at this death-watch beetle. And this dry rot in the main

157

beam. . . ." He began pulling the main beam away in handfuls. "This I know *all* about. Our greenhouses at home are an endless battle—'cause of the damp from the plants. Drives my father nuts . . . some tomato growers have the new aluminum greenhouses—they're great. But my old man's a stinge—he keeps on patching and propping up our old wooden ones. One day they'll fall down around his head burying him in tomato chutney up to his neck."

Simon gave a sudden explosive giggle. At the idea of the solemn, bald, ponderous Mr. la Chard buried in chutney up to his neck.

But the giggle choked off halfway. Tris gave him another funny look.

"My throat," mumbled Simon.

Then the two doors downstairs banged shut, one after the other.

They looked at each other. Simon got the impression that there was more going on in Tris's head than Tris was letting on.

"I'll just go and get my pistol," said Tris.

Simon waited.

Tris came back whistling; leaving both the doors open again.

"Wind blew them shut," he explained. He was carrying the pistol in his right hand. Had he loaded it downstairs?

The doors banged shut again.

Then the mill was full of noises. Whispers. Clicks. Bangs. Everywhere. But you couldn't place them in the shadows. The main beam, the one with dry-rot in it, groaned overhead.

Then a noise like a boy rattling an iron bar along iron

railings. And a rumble deeper and lower down than your own heart.

Creak, creak to their right; *crack, crack, crack* to their left.

And then all the main drive-shafts were turning; the great mill stone rumbling and sparking in its heavy bed.

The whole mill was a great drum with twenty insane drummers. Simon and Tris shouted at each other and heard nothing.

If someone came now, they would hear nothing. . . .

Tris turned and ran upstairs. Simon followed him, blundering, stumbling, blind.

Tris reached the top platform, and looked down at the sluice. Sluice pumping black water.

"Sluice-gate's worked itself loose," yelled Tris. "Things do that. . . . My father's greenhouse ventilators. . . ." He pulled the lever. Slowly the mill stopped.

"Let's go," said Simon, blundering toward the stair. He had a certain conviction now that when they got outside, the scarecrows would be waiting.

"No," said Tris. "Hang on. This is *great*."

He pulled the lever the other way. The mill started up again.

"*Whoom, whoom*," said Tris, with great enthusiasm. And opened up the lever a little bit more.

The mill went faster and faster. Rising in tone, up, up, up to a many-voiced chorus.

"Blast-off!" shrieked Tris, and threw the lever wide.

The mill roared; and began to moan inside its roaring. Agony inside the power. A horse being ridden to death. A pleading, pleading, *pleading*, inside the wood and the metal and the stone. *Please stop. Please, please don't wreck me.*

"That'll do," said Tris, and turned it off. The mill sighed and slowly settled. The last few turns were almost a gasp of relief.

As the noise ceased, Simon realized his head was clear as a bell. He knew the scarecrows were still lying in the field, where Tris had left them. Afraid to move. For some reason, afraid of Tris. *Why?*

"I'm hungry," complained Tris. "What time do your lot have lunch?"

Simon looked at his watch, dazed. It was nearly one o'clock.

"We'd better hurry," he said. "Or we'll be late."

On the way down, Tris paused to examine a crack in one of the whitewashed walls. He whistled. "That's new." He pulled flaking bits of whitewash from the edges of the crack. "You can see bloody daylight through it. This mill, old lad, has not got long for this world. Poor thing."

But there wasn't any regret in his voice.

They crossed the turnip field. The scarecrows were lying just as they'd left them.

"*Nasty* things," said Tris. And gave Starkey a flying kick where his ribs should have been.

"Hey, steady!" said Simon.

"Why?" asked Tris heartlessly.

"There's an old vicar watches this field. . . ."

"Good morning, vicar," yelled Tris at the top of his voice. "My uncle's a vicar, the old fraud. We shall now sing Hymn 256."

They traveled home to the sound of "Jesus wants me for a sunbeam."

160

"More potatoes, Tris?" Mum smirked. Like she thought he was God or something. "What have you two been doing this morning?"

"Been to that mill."

"Oh, that," said Mum. "We got the cats there."

"And I suppose you buy your flour at the pet shop?" asked Tris.

Joe Moreton laughed so much he splattered runner beans all over the tablecloth. Tris picked up the bits.

"You're supposed to *eat* those," he said to Joe, reprovingly.

Joe blew out a second mouthful, choked, had to be banged on the back and said to Tris, "You'll be the death of me. Do you *never* stop?"

"Only in Lent," said Tris. "And then only for five minutes."

Joe was smirking at him fatuously too. And Jane slipped her arm through Tris's slyly; from where she sat next to him at table.

"I *love* you, Tris," she said. With maddening predictability.

Oh, they were all so busy loving each other so much. It made Simon feel like a dull black shadow, who shouldn't be there. His mum, his sister, his mum's husband . . . what was so marvelous about Tris anyway?

"What did you make of the mill, Tris?" asked Joe Moreton.

"It's knackered," said Tris. "Cracks in the wall you could put your hand through. It'll go down bang, one of these days."

Helped along by Tris la Chard, thought Simon bitterly.

Don't bother telling them you nearly ran the thing to pieces.

"A real death-trap," said Joe, sagely. "It should be pulled down. If kids got to play in there . . . I think I'll ring up the council. It's their responsibility. They have a thing called a Compulsory Demolition Order."

"That would be a shame," said Mum. "It's a fascinating old place—a real relic. There aren't many water mills left. They ought to give it to the National Trust. I wonder who owns it."

"Well, actually, I think it might be us. When I bought this house at the auction, I rather think there was a bit more land across the field . . . and a mention of out-buildings. I got this place so damned cheap . . . and was so busy doing it up . . . I'll check. The National Trust can certainly have it for me . . . can't stand the place."

"Can I help you look it up?" asked Tris. "I'm rather interested. If it's going to be saved, you better get crack-ing." His voice sounded serious, suddenly, even urgent. Simon wondered why.

"We'll do it after lunch," said Joe. "Come up to my studio. You want to come, Simon?"

"No thanks," said Simon ungraciously. Why hadn't Joe asked *him* first?

"I'd like to come too," said Mum.

"And me," said Jane.

They made it sound like a bloody birthday party.

After the washing up, Simon slouched off into the gar-den in disgust. He looked over the gate into the turnip field. He knew what he would see.

Somebody had put the scarecrows back upright. And somebody had put Starkey's hat back on. And they had definitely been moved nearer.

Who had moved them?

And then he could no longer kid himself.

I have moved them, he thought. I open the door. I give them the power. Every time I let the devils in.

That is why they are afraid of Tris.

Tris can undo devils. That night in the dorm with Harris. . . .

There was the creaking of an axle, from the lane. And the sound of an organ on the march.

> *Lee-heed kindly light, amidst the encircling gloom*
> *Lee-heed thou me on. . . .*

Mercyfull the merciless. Who could deal wi' foxes, lazy horses and even the late Lord Herdsmere, Lord Knutsford's son. Mercyfull would know how to deal wi' a pack o' scarecrows. Mercyfull was afraid of nowt. Mercyfull the invincible, who cured headaches by running head down into marble fireplaces.

The gate crashed open.

"Mr. Mercyfull," called Simon. "Can you come here a minute?" He tried to make his voice calm, matter-of-fact, boyish.

Mercyfull seemed reluctant to come over; seemed inclined to sit on his wheelbarrow instead.

"Mr. *Mercyfull.*"

Slowly, the old man dragged himself over. Simon stepped on one side and pointed across the field to the scarecrows, and carefully watched Mr. Mercyfull's face. He imagined him saying, "I lined up all three wi' me gun, and got all three with one barrel. . . ."

But the old man merely stared a long time, then took out a red spotted handkerchief, wiped his face, and went back to his wheelbarrow. He suddenly looked rather ill.

"Do you recognize them?" asked Simon.

"Aye."

"The young miller, Josie Cragg and Starkey."

"Aye." The word was pulled out of the very depths of him.

"They've come back."

"Aye."

"How do I stop them?"

There was a long, long silence. A silence that seemed to go on forever. Then Mercyfull cocked his head on one side, as if consulting his repertoire, and began,

"It was the Fust War that finished hosses. Afore t'war there was thousands. Town councils used to pay fellers just to keep streets clear of hoss manure. But all t'hosses went to France an' none ever came back. France were death to a hoss—for every one killed by shot or shell, ten died o' underfeeding or overwok or pneumonia or just brok their hearts. Hoss traders hated sendin' hosses to France, no matter what t'Army paid. . . ."

"Mr. Mercyfull . . . the scarecrows . . . what do I *do* about them?"

"Had a lovely hoss once—thowt so much on her, I walked her all the way home from Oswestry hoss fair—all o' seventy mile an' it took me a day and a night. I'd just got her into stable an' rubbed her down—"

"Mr. Mercyfull . . . the scarecrows. . . ."

"When I seen t'hoss-requisitioning officer coming, I jacked the price sky high 'cause I didna want to part wi' her. . . ."

Simon grabbed the old arms, the horny hands, and tried

to pull Mr. Mercyfull out of the wheelbarrow by main force. He must help, he *must*.

"The officer—Captain Smith was his name—he weren't a bad feller . . . he only had one arm an' one eye on account o' the war. . . ."

Simon looked at him. His eyes were far away, cocked up somewhere into the sky. He droned on his set piece as if he was a record player . . . he was like the people who came back from Granny's funeral. All pretending to be jolly, and wondering who was next for the chop.

Simon walked away, equally blind. For the first time he knew there was no hope at all.

17

"No BREAD LEFT again," said Cosima. "*And* I've had to triple me order for fruit pies. *Triple!* I feel *raped!*"

She cast her eyes around her shop; hand to haggard face. There wasn't much on the shelves, apart from packets of disposable diapers, aerosols of instant starch, and some wizened apples looking very sorry for themselves.

And although there was still some pleasure in Cosima's voice when she said "raped," there wasn't much. She looked exhausted; a tiny nervous tic made her plucked eyebrow tremble. And she was resting on a high stool behind the counter, that had never been there before.

"You kids," said Cosima. "What have you started?"

Simon shrugged bad-temperedly. He hadn't started anything. It was Tris la Chard and Joe Moreton, the Dynamic Duo.

Discovering that Joe did own the mill, they had rung the local representative of the National Trust. Who happened to be a Knutsford architect. Who ummed, aahed, strode around the mill and declared it definitely thirteenth century (at least in the lower parts), which made it the oldest surviving water mill in the country. . . . And he whistled when he saw the cracks in the walls.

"They've got worse recently, *very* recently," he pronounced.

Apparently the situation was critical; a national treasure hung in the balance. Tris la Chard nodded intelligently, keeping his face absolutely straight.

By the evening, there were three more architects crawling all over it, bickering about transome and architrave, Early English and Norman. Next day there were ten architects, including several from Manchester, and half the County Planning department. And the next day the big National Trust boys from London. . . .

But at least in the beginning, all the talk was of rescue work, conservation. Even when the Granada van pulled up by the house and technicians began paying out black cables across the turnip field. Followed quickly by their rivals from *Look North*. Everybody in the house crowded round the telly that night.

It was unfortunate that Robin Smart, driven out of the mill by National Trust protests, chose to give his commentary against the background of the scarecrows. . . .

That was the first time They got into Mill House.

Nobody seemed to notice, except Simon.

And perhaps Tris la Chard, Simon thought, watching his inscrutable face in the flickering light from the screen.

And Jane, who said proudly, "Those are *our* scare-crows!"

But by the following day, some reporter on the *Knuts-ford Guardian* had dug up the old story of the murder at the mill. The day after that, the national press descended. It was a marvelous story for the Silly Season of August, when nothing else was happening. And on Sunday, the *News of the World* and *The People* made full-page spreads of the Murder at the Mill. There were smudgy wartime photos of the miller (whose name turned out to have been George Joseph Henshaw), glowering stubbornly out of page five, unsure of himself as ever.

Josie Cragg lived again, with the collar of her gray tweed coat turned up and her legs crossed for the photographer's benefit. Raising a glass of something or other, to a grinning U.S. serviceman.

Starkey's picture was from a police photograph; it made him look dead and decapitated. But worse, the closer you looked, the more it broke down into spots and patches of light and dark. You still couldn't see the real Starkey, as you could see the real miller and the real Josie Cragg.

There were reporters everywhere, digging up old gran-nies who'd been at school with Josie; or the miller's first sweetheart. If it could be believed, the miller had fallen in love with a whole platoon of land-girls. And Josie's class at the village school must have been full to bursting.

But nobody had known Starkey.

The TV vans came back again, churning the village green to pulp, and twice knocking over the small war me-morial. Mill House had been under siege; after two days Joe had forbidden anyone to give another interview, but

167

none of them could go out into the garden without a flash-bulb going off, and cameras clicking. . . .

"Rape!" repeated Cosima, as a new customer came in, only to be turned away breadless. "Rape. I think they should knock that rotten old place down. And I wish some-one would take those Great Nasty Things away." She meant the scarecrows, and there was a certain desperation in her voice.

Simon drifted out to the sound of long explanations why there would be no more Arctic Rolls till the middle of next week. Went back to his own garden and looked over into the turnip field.

The turnips had suffered. There was now a motorway of mashed turnip-pulp where the old path had been. For fifty yards on each side, the turnips were stripped of leaves, sticking mute white stumps into the air.

How many gawping sightseers, how many landrovers, how many black cables transmitting power?

Devastation everywhere, except where the scarecrows stood. They held their ground defiantly, unscathed. The footmarks went straight toward them, then circled left or right, giving them a wide berth. Somehow, no snaking cable had caught and toppled them; no turning van backed into them. They just stood, watching Mill House.

And at night, when the vans had gone and the reporters were packing the pub, the scarecrows moved nearer. Each night they seemed to get more powerful. It was as if they were drawing power from the electric cables, the smell of diesel fumes; above all, from the fuss on the telly. It was funny. Every telly cameraman who came to the mill seemed to have his eye caught by them; would use up his last few

168

feet of film on them, on his way back to the van and home. The news editors obviously liked them too; they would suddenly appear in the last few seconds of any telly coverage. But the announcer would never say anything about them. Only Jane would, as she compulsively watched every broadcast.

"Those are *our* scarecrows."

Until Simon could have screamed.

And the scarecrows got into the newspapers too, that now lay scattered by Jane all over the lounge floor, as she made her scarecrow scrapbook, under the flickering blue light of the telly.

Oh, They were inside the house now, all right. More and more real all the time.

What, thought Simon, had Tris thought he was doing, getting Joe to publicize the mill? Had he thought, by making it public property, to weaken its power, spread it to the four winds? Had he hoped to "blow," to expose the scarecrows as if they were enemy spies?

Well, it hadn't worked. They'd thrived on it.

On the other hand, the family at Mill House got less and less real. To the reporters they said the same things over and over again. Joe, making the same wise-sounding pronouncement about a Medieval Gem and a Gift to the Nation. Mum, saying bravely she didn't mind sleeping in a room where a murderer had slept; it didn't bother her at all. Jane being endlessly coy and flirty in return for sweets. Even Tris's jokes got repetitive. And having said all these things in real life, they said them again from the flickering screen.

Mr. Mercyfull's daughter brought a message that her dad

was poorly. She lingered on the doorstep of Mill House, a plain middle-aged countrywoman, and said that at his time of life, what could you expect? And Simon had known he wouldn't see Mr. Mercyfull again.

Only Simon didn't talk to anybody. It took all his time and energy bearing it, while the walls of Mill House seemed to get thinner and thinner and the scarecrows nearer and nearer. He was waiting again. Waiting and very tired, and very far away.

When would it happen? When the newsmen finally went away? When Tris la Chard went home?

Jane seldom went out any more; even she was tired of newsmen now. She just watched the telly, thumb in mouth, pulled in on herself.

Joe and Mum didn't talk much at the table either. But one night after Tris and Simon and Jane had gone to bed, they had a blazing row, because Joe hadn't been able to paint that day because the telephone never stopped ringing. Mum said he'd better bugger off to London then, and leave her to face the music alone. And Joe said if that was the way she felt, he might just do that. They'd never quarreled before. Their voices echoed and echoed around Mill House, as Simon and Tris lay in bed and listened.

Simon was shocked; but only in a far-off way. Somehow it didn't really sound like Joe and Mum at all. . . .

Not from where he was hovering, on the gray edge of sleep.

18

It HAPPENED on the Tuesday night.

Everybody got frenetically high over dinner. Just like at Granny's funeral again. . . .

Joe telling vulgar stories about being a guttersnipe in the slums of Salford, and Tris just couldn't get enough of it. Traitor.

And Jane, the other little traitor, hanging onto Joe's arm, warming herself as if he was a radiator. Looking from Tris to Joe. Sitting between them, squealing with delight. Until Simon could have cheerfully strangled her.

And Mum smiling, smiling. Giving them all that big, warm, loving smile that she used to save for Simon alone.

All the smiling traitors; forgetting Father. Who had been brave and was now so lonely, in the graveyard in Aden. As if he had never been. . . .

Oh, they'll pay, thought Simon. But he went on smiling at the jokes, joining in the fun. So that even Mum was fooled, and pleased.

"What shall we *play* tonight?" asked Joe archly.

"Ghosts, Joe. Monsters!" yelled Jane. "Like at Hallowe'en."

"Who'll be the *ghost*? *Who'll* be the monster?" asked Joe, glaring at her, hunching his back like the Hunchback of Notre Dame, and trying to brush his scanty hair down over his eyes.

Jane gave a delighted shudder, and clung to him. "*You* be the monster; an' I'll be the baby monster an' ride on your back." She began hunching her shoulders too, and pulling terrible faces at everybody.

171

"You be careful," said Mum. "Or your face will stay like that! And if you're both going to be monsters, who's going to be haunted? There's no point in being ghosts if there's nobody to haunt. Shall I be the one to be haunted?"

"No. You're the mummy-monster. We'll be mummy, daddy and baby monsters."

"You can haunt me," said Tris. "Will I do?" He ruffled Jane's hair.

Jane thought hard. "It's a pity. 'Cause you'd make a good monster too. I think you'd make a *lovely* monster."

"It's being so handsome that does it," said Tris. "Compliments will get you everywhere. Anyway, *somebody's* got to be haunted."

"Yes," said Jane regretfully. "Somebody has."

"You can haunt me as well," said Simon. Something spiteful escaped into his voice, so Jane looked at him, frowning, baffled.

"Oh, all right then," she said, suddenly cross. Then she turned away to Joe. "Shall we have the ghost music? Lights out an' everything?"

"Shhh," said Joe. "You mustn't give away trade secrets, or I'll have to report you to the Monsters' Union."

Joe and Jane bustled off; you could hear scurrying upstairs, and cupboard doors opening and shutting, and her high-pitched giggle. So high-pitched that Mum called up the stairs, "Steady, Joe—don't get her too worked up." But her voice was loving, not cross. Then she said, "I'll do the dishes."

"I'll do them if you like," said Tris. "Don't you want to get ready too?"

"Oh, mummy-monsters don't get a moment to turn

round. They always have to get ready at the last possible moment . . . hardly time to put on their blood-lipstick. These dishes won't take me long." And she departed briskly with the trolley.

Those about to be haunted sat on at the table, listening to the noises in the rest of the house, which seemed unnaturally loud in a surrounding silence. Dishes clinking in the kitchen. The record player being tried, then as suddenly turned off, so that it only played five notes, and Simon couldn't make out what record they were trying.

The lights went on and off several times experimentally; then violently off and on, over and over again, as Jane got her hands on the main switch.

Mum yelled upstairs, "Stop that, you two! You'll blow the fuses."

"So-rry," Joe yelled back. He sounded about seven years old himself, poor deluded fool.

Simon and Tris didn't look at each other, or say anything.

At least, Tris kept looking at Simon; but Simon wouldn't look back. Just went on playing with the few things Mum had left on the dining table. One clean knife, two clean forks, a serving spoon and a plate with half a bread roll.

Simon's left hand played with the roll, tearing it cleverly apart one-handed. Rolling the pieces into fat little balls between finger and thumb. When he had made four, he stopped and looked at them.

Two big fat balls, one medium-sized ball, and a small one.

Viciously he stubbed them flat onto the plate, one after the other.

"I think you'd better go and be a monster as well," said Tris quietly. From his very tone, Simon knew that Tris had guessed everything. But Simon said, enjoying his own cruel insincerity, "I can't leave you to be haunted alone."

With that phrase, he killed his friendship with Tris. Some last loyalty broke.

Tris understood. That was the awful thing. Tris understood, and yet he would not let Simon go. His own half of the friendship remained intact; just sad. He said again. "You go and be a monster with the others, Simon. I'll survive being haunted alone. In fact, if you go and be a monster with the others, I'm quite sure we'll *all* survive. . . ."

"No," said Simon. His voice was like a slash at a rope; the rope of friendship.

But again the rope of Tris's friendship didn't break.

"Everybody read-dy?" called Joe coyly from upstairs.

"Just let me comb my hair," said Mum, coming out of the kitchen and undoing her apron. "I've got to look my worst." She went upstairs too.

"Don't *do* it, Simon," said Tris, very quietly. He went to the dining room window, the one that faced the turnip field, and pulled the curtains half back.

All Simon could see was the reflection of the triple light-fitting in the window glass.

But Tris said, "They're there. They're right against the hedge."

Simon said nothing. But they both knew he knew what Tris meant.

"Take *coverrrr!*" sang out Joe. Here we *co-ome*. Last *waaarning!*"

Jane was splitting herself with glee, and Mum was whispering she mustn't. She must be a *proper* monster.

174

Then the lights slowly faded. Joe had done a lot of light-and-sound work as an art student; and he had the house rigged with remote-control dimmers, extra loudspeakers and all kinds of electronic jiggery-pokery. He let the lights dim, until you despaired of them; then brightened them back to hope, then let you drop into total darkness.

First the lights went out in the dining room, but stayed on in the hall. Then they dimmed in the hall, but flickered lightning-blue in the kitchen. The whole house felt like a dazed, dying body; disorientated, struggling to go on living.

Joe was good, a good artist; Simon gave him that. It helped, all Joe's great creative mind. It was helping to destroy him, and the fool didn't even know it.

Then the record player started playing, big, wild. A cool detached part of Simon's brain noted it was Wagner's *Ride of the Valkyrie*.

Corny. But effective. The feel of galloping; the feel of something *coming*. Louder and louder. Nearer and nearer. Calling, summoning, summoning.

Dee-dum ditty deeedum, deedum ditty deeeedum.

Then the tune dragged weirdly, then swelled to an impossible loudness, that threatened to explode the amplifiers. There was a startled shout from Joe.

He hadn't planned *that* one. You could hear him swearing in the dark, groping for the controls of the record player. But the controls made no difference. The music slammed and bellowed round the hall and corridors now of its own accord, like a living gale.

Then stopped abruptly. But things were moving in the air; little flickers in the corner of the eye. Among the half-lights and moving, living shadows, things were *coming*.

But the mob upstairs still hadn't noticed, stupid fools.

175

"Whoo-hooo-hooo-hooooooooh!" Joe's voice, very deep from his deep chest, basso-profundo like Chaliapin in a Russian opera.

"Whooo-hooooo-hooooo-hooo!" went Jane, very shrill and collapsing into giggles.

"Whoo-hooo-hooooh," went Mum, very lost and feeble.

"I come, I come, I cooooome!" roared Joe.

Bump, bump, drag, drag went his feet on the stairs. Like Quasimodo or Dracula or Frankenstein.

"I'm slipping!" complained Jane. "Hold me *tighter.*"

Simon sensed Tris move in the dark; looked in his direction. Tris was listening. But not toward the silly fools outside the dining room door. He was listening, ear cocked, at the gap in the curtain over the window.

He *knew*. . . .

And then, everything went black. The record player screeched up to an agonizing crescendo, and died for good, with a long-drawn-out groan.

"What the hell . . . ?" said Joe, suddenly very surprised and un-monster, every inch the careful householder. "What the hell . . . main fuse, I suppose. Oh, damn!"

"Mend it!" squealed Jane. "Mend it quick, Joe. I'm *frightened.*"

But all their voices were wobbling and fading, like voices under water.

Then a deep voice shouted,

"I will be maister in my own house!"

A deep voice, like Joe's. But not Joe's.

And suddenly the air was filled with the sweet warm smell of whiskey; whisky on the breath.

And a strange male smell; dirty, middle-aged, alien.

176

Simon disliked it; disliked having any strange man in the house near his mother. That was the first thing he disliked about what was happening. . . .

"I *will* be maister in my own house."

"Sit down, you old fool. You *are* maister. What you going on about?"

"I'm *not* maister. Starkey's maister now. Where is he? I'll mark him. I'll mark him and I'll mark thee too, see if I don't!"

"Let me go, you old fool." Then there was a storm of voices, blurring and booming and fading, as if the air was full of rags. And the female voice, yelling, "Starkey, Starkey, come quick!"

All getting nearer. Along the narrow upstairs corridor; down the dark stairs. Everywhere.

Simon could not move. He was paralyzed by the smell of the strange man; only there were two smells of two strange men now; and the air was full of a struggling gasping and straining.

Then he sensed Tris slide past him in the dark; heard Tris slam the dining room door and lock it. The voices faded, but did not stop; the whole house was full of them, except the dining room. It was like being in a little hut with a great gale blowing outside.

"Well, you've done it," said Tris calmly.

"Yes," said Simon. Only now he could think of nothing but that Mum was out there somewhere. Or what was left of her. She seemed agonizingly precious, now that she was gone.

What were they *doing* to Mum . . . ?

"It may not be too late," said Tris.

177

"It is too late." Simon was feeling horrible; horrified yet fascinated, like when he'd watched a spider trap and kill a fly.

"They've come for you too," said Tris. "You made *four* balls of bread. . . ."

"The fourth one was *you*."

"Oh no it wasn't. What have I got to do with all this? I belong to a mum and dad in Jersey, and miles and miles of tomato plants. What *you're* doing is all yours. Those murders . . . the son died too—broke his neck riding a horse two months later . . . I read it up in the back files at the *Knutsford Guardian* office. *They* tricked you, Simon."

"Oh, God, what can I do?"

"Only you know. You made all this. You can break it. You may still be in time. I don't think They've finished yet. . . ."

"How?"

"Window."

Tris flung the curtains back, and opened the window.

"Run, Simon, run!"

Run, Simon, run. Like on the rugby field. All the kids, all the masters shouting, and the ball in his hands.

He ran. Smashed through the hedge as if it was a rugby pack. Felt the branches clutch at his shirt and tear away despairingly.

He darted between the figures of the scarecrows. Starkey was still lurking at the back. He almost ran into him, into the filthy smell of rotting straw; but swerved just in time. The turnip leaves, full of rain, lashed his ankles like whips and threw wet up his trousers. He trampled on the rounded bodies of the turnips as if he was in a black room full of hard solid rugby balls.

178

He didn't run for help to the village. *He* had the ball; nobody else could carry it now. He was alone. Nobody backing up. This was how it felt to be alone. Not terrible, but marvelous. This was how Father must have felt, driving his jeep at the Flossies. . . . Father hadn't really been lonely. He'd simply been *alone*. He felt one with his father at last. *Head straight for what you're scared of, Simon. It'll usually run away, if you do. If not, you're no worse off. . . .* With Father there, he no longer cared if he lived or died.

He was panting now; great gouts of breath. Panting in total darkness, but still running, running for the mill. And somehow he knew, in all that turnip-filled darkness, just exactly where the mill was. If he was tied beyond hope to the mill, the mill was also tied beyond hope to him. It couldn't escape him, no more than he could escape it.

Run straight at your enemy. And, in running, gasping, falling and getting up, he became aware of some kind of power in himself. When he got to the mill, he would know what to do. He knew that; and somehow the mill knew it too. Somehow, he sensed the mill was afraid; and that made his legs strong.

He was running head down. Something—maybe the end of the turnips—made him look up. Just in time. He teetered on the very brink of the mill dam. One more step and he would have been into the mill pool, where the sides were too high to climb out, and he would have sunk down through the sooty depths, into the gray scummy arms of the weed.

Hard *luck!* He flung the thought at the mill, wolfishly. Turned left and ran along the dam wall. The smell of the pool came up to his nostrils. But the pool was too late to catch him now.

Down the steps past the mill race. It gaped at his feet in

the dark, waiting for him. It was as if his feet were running on a knife edge.

But he ran true. The door smashed open as he hit it. Splintered more easily than he expected it to.

Wood splintering . . . *smash, smash, smash.*

He ran through the living room, sending table and chair crashing in the dark.

Smash, smash. SMASH. Smash wood.

He fought his way upstairs. Ropes snatched at his face, strong, thick and hairy. He ran into the hanging sack, dangling heavy over its trapdoor. He felt his feet teetering on sharp stair edges, over pits of dark. For a dreadful second he thought he was going to run round and round forever, like a rat in a maze, a hamster in a cage.

And then he was on the top landing, and there was enough pale moonlight now, coming through the slatted window, for him to see the starting-lever that controlled the sluice.

There is moonlight, he thought, far away. There is moonlight. And he grabbed the handle and heaved.

He was too weak. His hands were too slippery. It would *never* move.

He gathered his body for a last rush; hit the lever with shoulder behind hand and body behind shoulder and legs behind body. The wooden lever bit into him like a death-blow with a sword. He felt his flesh crushed, his bone bitten.

It did not move.

He threw himself again; and again. Each time the wooden sword entered him and he died a little.

There was not enough of him left for a fourth blow. He was beaten. But all about him was a rushing, and sluicing, a thumping. A grinding of cogs, like a boy rattling an iron bar

180

along iron railings. A pounding like a great heart, like two great hearts, three. Another boy began to rattle a bar along another railing. Everywhere around him, the mill woke to life.

But it must wake to death. The hearts must pound to death; the boys with iron bars must run till they died.

He pushed the handle of the sluice down as far as it would go. It moved easily now. The noise increased. But he waited until every sound said danger and destruction.

Only then did he run. Only then did he seek to save himself. The mill was full of blue moonlight now. Great cogs swung out at him. Rows of gallows in stark, never-ending succession. All building up the screaming in the wood, the torture in the ill-greased axles. He had never heard such a noise. A hundred drums were reverberating up through the soles of his feet, the palms of his hands on the handrails. And all the time the thrumming climbed in intensity, like the thrumming in a taut-drawn crossbow, or a rope just before it snaps. A harp of tension.

The soles of his feet told him he had reached cold, solid ground. As always, his body told him which way to run. He went through the living room again, as if it, too, were a rugby-scrum. Not that he couldn't see the scattered furniture now, in the moonlight, but he knew from the crescendo-ing noise behind him that he had no time to run around it. His foot caught in the rungs of the overturned chair. The wood was dry, light, rotten. He kicked his foot as he might kick a ball, and the chair flew into the whitewashed wall and fell in worm-eaten fragments.

He crashed into the table and drove it right across the room with his thighs; the edge bit into his muscles like another wooden blade.

And then he was through the door and only the long dead grass was sifting gently round him, as if it loved him.

There came a crack that made him turn. Then a series of sounds like sheet lightning. A whole snapped beam of timber, sharp as a lance, speared upward through the roof, sending a patch of tiles up into the air like birds. The windows burst out in hails of shining silver like snowflakes.

And then the roof fell in. For a moment the gable ends towered clean against the sky like bishops' miters, and then they too fell inward. Water spurted, bursting out, finding new channels, making new waterfalls that changed under his very eyes as more and more of the mill fell. Every time masonry choked it, the water burst out again into a new place. There were pools forming, through which great bubbles of cloudy, floury air burst out, as if something was drowning. And then, with a last rumble, the mill dam itself was breached; the wheel fell, and water covered everything in a huge, spreading black pool that lapped gently around Simon's feet. The bubbles and ripples continued a long time, and then were still.

In the silence, in a wood near, a night-jar began to call.

Simon sighed with a deep satisfaction. Whether Mum and Jane were safe or dead, nobody could ever take away from him the fall of the mill. It was a fact, solid as Father's death. All life was changed.

As he turned away, not thinking where he was going—a turning-away and not a turning-toward—he saw Them. On the skyline; on this edge of the turnip field.

He was very weary. He would almost certainly lose. But it didn't matter. He had learned the secret. Make straight for your enemy.

They looked very big as he climbed slowly toward them. Big and very black. But long before he reached them, he noticed a difference. They sagged, two to the left, one to the right, on the very point of falling. One puff of wind, one small bird perching, would have done for any of them. Yet they clung to a kind of life. He knew that with the mill gone, they were finished. With the mill gone, they could never come again. Their home, their heart, was gone.

Yet still they wished to be. What there was left, clung on and lived in the ragged forms.

It made it a very satisfying pleasure . . . and yet he could not begin. Wearily, the four figures stood and surveyed each other, like punch-drunk boxers.

He might have stood all night; he might have stood forever, if he hadn't thought of Mum; Mum getting out of the Morris, her hair short, red and shining; saying hallo and smiling and not even asking how he was. Mum must be avenged.

He grasped the shoulders of the miller and wrenched with both hands. There was a very slight resistance, a very, very slight resistance, and then the cloth of the coat tore and tore. Once started, the miller went as swiftly as his mill.

And it was the thought of Jane, kneeling, poking into a puddle with a stick and singing to herself that did for the miller's wife.

But he stood a long time in front of Starkey. Who would he avenge on Starkey? It was very important to know who he would avenge on Starkey.

Tris? No. Not on. Starkey, whatever had happened, could have done nothing to Tris. Tris belonged with the acres of tomatoes, on Jersey.

183

Who then?

And then he remembered Joe; not Joe drawing his sarcastic cartoons, or standing coolly making his snide remarks at the private view, but Joe working from a life-model, face wrinkled up with concentration, swaying backward and forward in an agony of thought, bumping backward with a start into the old painty cupboard, and then finally making a tiny blue cross on the canvas.

Joe had a right to live too. Not, maybe, a right to Mum, Jane, Tris. But a right to live.

Starkey fell as Simon's hand touched him; he had been the most rotted of the lot.

Finally, a watcher below might have seen the fourth figure, smaller than the rest but almost as tattered, fall to the ground beside them.

Something tickled Simon's nose. Something gentle, without meaning. Something that smelled green, moist and good. He moved his hand to push it away, and grasped a turnip leaf.

He opened his eyes. He lay inside a green tunnel of turnip leaves. He sat up with an ouch, and broke surface into a golden mist of sunrise. On all sides, the turnips faded into the mist. The turnip leaves talked quietly to each other, as the wind blew waves across them, turning them purple, then silver. There was nothing in the world but turnips, and home.

And then he saw three figures coming at him through the mist. They approached very slowly; edges vague and blurred.

The one in front was a big, big man. The second, smaller, moved like a woman. And the third, a fair way behind, was a smaller man. . . .

184

A moan broke from him.

He had not destroyed them after all. Once called, they had become indestructible. He put his face in his hands and waited for the unthinkable end.

And then there was a noise; an old familiar noise.

"Wait for me. Please, Joe, *wait* for me. I'm tired. I'm all *wet*."

He raised his eyes, scarcely daring to hope. A fourth, tiny figure was emerging out of the mist, behind the other three.

"Simon?" said Joe.

"*Simon*. We've been worried *sick*. We've been searching for you *everywhere*," said Mum.

"Hallo, you great turnip," said Tris la Chard.